Jarek Tomszak

THE EDEN EVACUATION

The Greatest Art Forgery Ever Dreamed

AUSTIN MACAULEY PUBLISHERS™

LONDON • CAMBRIDGE • NEW YORK • SHARJAH

Ordering Information
Quantity sales: Special discounts are available on quantity purchases by corporations, associations, and others. For details, contact the publisher at the address below.

Publisher's Cataloging-in-Publication data
Tomszak, Jarek
The Eden Evacuation

ISBN 9798891550100 (Paperback)
ISBN 9798891550117 (ePub e-book)

Library of Congress Control Number: 2023922725

www.austinmacauley.com/us

First Published 2024
Austin Macauley Publishers LLC
40 Wall Street, 33rd Floor, Suite 3302
New York, NY 10005
USA

mail-usa@austinmacauley.com
+1 (646) 5125767

I walk out of the cathedral into the hot bright square. Shouting tour guides are herding flocks of tourists. Sweaty farmers from a faraway land videotape every piece of the wall illuminated by the guide as they ecstatically grasp age-old stones. They are so caught up in capturing the moment that they have no time to experience it. They will see Italy when they return home, in the color of their moving pictures; pictures that will have nothing to do with reality.

Zbigniew Herbert-Barbarian in the Garden.

Adam and Gina

I

Gray dawn was entering through the window blinds. In the still fairly dark room, the only light was generated by the deemed blue digits of the clock. Adam in his sleep was turning in the bed, when suddenly for no reason he opened his eyes to the clock. The digits were blinking. Thoughts quickly ran through his mind: *Power went out and then came back, making the clock blink. What time is it?* He reached out for his cell phone nearby; it was fiSSSSve in the morning. The alarm had not yet gone off. Last night, to be safe, he set both alarms on the clock and the phone. Today, this morning he had to wake up on time. *I still have some time*, he thought.

At that moment he realized, it was no point going back to sleep, as there were less than thirty minutes left for the alarm to sound. He tossed around in the bed for a few minutes, and then at some point as he placed himself on his back, he started to think what would happen when he got out of bed… He'll get up, go to the bathroom, and get into the shower. Then he'll make a coffee. While the coffee is being made, he'll dress and then drink it. Then he'll get on the train which will take him to the airport, where he'll meet his girlfriend and will fly to Italy…

As premeditated, he was taking a shower and for some reason, he recalled a dream he had last night, which he realized by now, was a cause he woke up before the alarm went off. In his dream, he was in a cab going to the airport, running late for his flight. The cab driver took an unusual route to the airport and seemed to be lost, although he claimed he knew what he was doing. Adam tried to instruct the driver how to get to the correct route, but he would not listen. Finally, they arrived at the airport just as it was time to get on the plane and Adam worried that he might not make it through the security check on time and Gina would go without him. He got to the gate and found out that no one had got on that plane yet, as it was delayed. But he could not find Gina among the passengers. She was not there. That's when he woke up.

Weird. I'm not taking a cab to the airport, he thought, shutting off the water.

When he arrived at the airport, Gina was not there, but he was not worried. She lived in the suburbs, and it could take a longer time to get to O'Hare and there was still plenty of time. He looked around. People were moving in all directions. Some were walking slowly, sort of scoping around. Some were almost running not paying attention to anybody or anything. And some just walked at a steady pace and seemed to be most accustomed to this environment.

Adam pulled out his phone and sent a text, "I'm at the airport. Where are you?"

In a second, he received a reply. "Right, behind you."

He turned around and there was Gina, right where she said. She was a blonde girl with hair reaching just to her shoulders and big, dark eyes. Standing next to Adam she didn't seem to be as tall as she really was. Adam was a tall and athletic man of some Nordic, Scandinavian descent. He looked like he might play basketball or volleyball. But the sport was not his thing.

They hugged and kissed.

"Hi babe, you just came in?" Adam asked putting his arm around her.

"Yeah, my cab just pulled in, when you were walking in," she answered.

"Let's eat something," proposed Adam.

"I'm not hungry, just had breakfast," she said.

"I didn't. Let me grab something. We've got plenty of time."

"Let's check-in and get through security first," Gina replied.

"Yeah, you're right. Lanes might be long."

Indeed, lanes were long, but even though they were moving fast and steady, waiting in them ate most of that plenty of time Adam thought they had. As they progressed to the gate, Adam stopped at a small sandwich shop and ordered some food. The first half of the sandwich, he ate on the way to the gate. When they arrived, people were not boarding the plane yet. They found two empty seats. As Adam was consuming the rest of his sandwich, he looked around. Almost everyone, including Gina, had their eyes glued to their phones, scrolling, reading, flipping through photographs, typing, and sending messages.

Soon after he finished his breakfast, it was time to board the plane.

As they settled down in their seats inside the plane, Adam pulled his tablet and said to Gina, "It's time to read now."

"What are you reading?" Gina asked.

"Something you don't have to. I suppose you already know this stuff."

"What is it?" She asked again.

"I'm reading about art," he answered and continued, "about Vatican Museum. So, I don't act like a fool when we get there. You know… You've just got your degree in that field," he added with a smile.

"Perhaps I should read it since museums seem to be more about history than art. And history is your domain. Also, I'm a painter, an artist."

"Sure, if you want to," replied Adam handing the tablet to Gina. "There is one piece of art there that I'm very interested in. I know all about it; I'm excited to see it up close. You have more appreciation for art than I do, so when we get there, you'll tell me what you think."

As Gina wanted to ask a question, she was interrupted by a flight attendant and asked to turn off the tablet, as they were getting ready for takeoff. Then safety procedures were shown on monitors and the captain announced, "Cabin crew, prepare for takeoff."

Once they were in the air, Gina turned on the tablet and opened a page with the painting, looked at it for a second, and said to Adam, "Tell me about it."

"About that painting?" Adam asked looking at the tablet in her hands.

"Yes."

"It's in Vatican's so-called Sobieski's Room. It's a huge painting showing Polish King Jan Sobieski dispatching a courier with a letter to the Pope after winning the Battle of Vienna in 1683. It was a battle that stopped the Turk Ottoman Empire's conquest of Europe. Turks conquered southeast Europe and the Balkans and were marching on Vienna. If Vienna had fallen, they would have had an open road to the rest of Europe and their ultimate goal—Rome. Islam would take over Christian Western civilization."

"It seems that history repeats itself these days," said Gina.

"Not quite," replied Adam. "Today, it's a different type of conquest of Europe, but the goal is the same."

"That's what I meant."

"At that time, Western Europe was weak and divided."

"Just like today," Gina interrupted again.

"Western powers needed help to stop Turks' expansion. So, the Pope was sending letters to one king asking him to come with aid—the Polish king. But Poland had its own problems with Turks on its eastern borders and the king... That's him..." Adam stopped and pointed to the picture, "...was not quick in responding to Pope's requests. Oh, how I wish, I could read those letters and other documents related to this. Most historians claim such letters don't exist and communication between the Pope and the king was done through other channels, like German, Austrian, and French dukes and barons. But I think there was a direct exchange in the form of letters, and they are locked somewhere in Vatican vaults."

"When Turks laid siege on Vienna," Adam continued, "Jan Sobieski assembled an army and marched to save the city. He won the battle. Turks retreated leaving everything behind. You know the date the battle ended?" He asked rhetorically and continued. "It was on the 11 September 1683," here he paused. "The painting was painted by a Polish painter in the nineteenth century, and it was presented to the Pope on the two hundred years anniversary of the battle. Poland was partitioned at that time and divided by the three empires. His paintings show the greatness of Poland that it was in the past, to keep Poles' spirit up in those dark times."

"Interesting," said Gina.

"Yeah, interestingly, the empires occupying Poland were Germany and Russia, and get this…" Adam paused for a second, "Austrian Empire, that's how Europe paid back Poles for saving its ass earlier. It's sad and ironic, isn't it? But the irony is bigger. The only country that did not acknowledge the partition of Poland was the Ottoman-Turk Empire."

As Adam finished his story, the stewardess was already offering drinks. He didn't order anything, and Gina had a cup of coffee.

"You read and I'll get some sleep. I didn't get much sleep last night. Went to bed kind of late and woke up before the alarm," he said as he recalled his strange dream, but he didn't mention it to Gina.

Adam closed his eyes, but the uncomfortable seat and the plane's engine noise coming into the cabin prevented falling asleep. He must have been tired because occasionally for short flashes of time, he slept, but as soon as his head fell forward, he'd wake up. It was irritating.

When they landed in Rome, he was really tired, but relieved at the same time.

"How do you feel?" He asked Gina when the plane was arriving at the gate.

"I'm so tired," she answered quickly.

"So am I. We'll get some sleep when we get to the hotel."

It was 2 a.m. when they dropped on the bed in the hotel. Even though it was only 6 p.m. in the States, the travel took its toll. They were exhausted and quickly fell asleep.

Adam, as he thought, felt heavy Gina's arm resting on his side. But deep in his sleep, he could not decide if it was in his dreams or something that was real. Still not sure of his dreams, he removed the arm to release the burden and as it seemed to him, he felt Gina was not pleased.

"Wake up," he seemed to hear the voice of Gina. Adam opened his eyes and for less than a second light became a calamity taking over his pupils. It was late morning.

"We didn't pull down window shades," said Adam still half asleep.

"Someone is knocking on the door," replied Gina.

Adam got up and walked to the door.

"Who is it?" He asked without opening the door.

"Cleaning," answered some woman with a heavy Russian accent.

Adam opened the door slightly and said, "Not now, please. We just woke up."

"Okay," the lady seemed to understand.

He closed the door and as he was walking back to the room, his eyes finally cleared.

"It's late. We're not going to make it to the Vatican Museum now. There are long lines to get tickets and we had to be there early in the morning, at least two hours ago," Adam said looking at Gina.

"Don't worry. We'll go there tomorrow," said Gina sitting up in the bed, and added, "you know, all that's there, it's been there for centuries. One more day is not going to make a difference." She paused and then said with a little smile:

"It's not going anywhere."

Adam smiled back.

"Okay, what now? Let's go out and get some breakfast. Italian coffee in a bistro?"

"How about shower first?" She almost laughed.

"We're not going to fit in that shower together," said Adam. "I was in that bathroom last night before sleep. It's tiny."

"Who said we're going there together?" Gina said smiling teasingly, jumping out of the bed and running to the bathroom. "It's mine now," she yelled closing the bathroom door.

"Shit. I was on my way there. How long it's going to take you?" He replied seriously and anxiously, as he was caught off guard and that really annoyed him.

Then he sat on the couch and yelled after a few minutes, "How long it's going to be?" He added after less than a minute. "I know we're on vacation, but we have some plans and schedules."

There was no response besides the sound of the water coming from the shower head in the bathroom, so he just thought to himself, *I have everything figured out, planned and there is no cooperation or even understanding, from anyone.* He added that as he recalled the email that he sent weeks ago to his old-time acquaintance who was a Catholic priest and got an assignment in the Vatican. In the email, he asked for some advice about Rome and the Vatican and hoped to meet, but got no answer yet.

An hour had already passed when Adam and Gina finally stood by the door, ready to go out. As Adam was reaching out to open it, sudden knocking suspended his action for a second. He opened the door, and the cleaning lady was there staring at them.

"We are leaving now. Yes, it's okay to clean now," said Adam after a second of hesitation and showed the lady into the room.

Walking down the short hallway, Gina asked, "Taking the stairs or the elevator?"

"Elevator?" Adam replied in surprise. "It's only a third floor," and added somehow triumphantly, "you didn't let me in the shower with you and now you want to get into the elevator that is as tiny as the shower cabin in our room?"

"Who said, we're getting into the elevator together?" She asked.

They both laughed walking down the stairs and kept laughing as they walked out into the street.

It was almost noon as they strolled down the hilly street, then turned and got to the bottom of the steep, narrow stairs. It was a hot day. Even though the stairs were steep and long, they decided to walk up, as the walls of the building on both sides shaded them. They stopped at the small bistro on the corner of a small square next to the top of the stairs and sat down outside at the table shaded by the umbrella. They were glad they took the stairs up, as the view from the place on part of the city below was incredible. Far in the distance, St. Peter's Basilica's dome was towering above the buildings around.

Not long after they sat down, the waiter showed up right by them. Young, tall guy with thick, long, black hair nicely combed.

"Two double espressos," said Adam.

"Certainly, any sugar?" The waiter answered with a British accent.

"Yes, please," answered Adam.

"Not for me," said Gina.

Waiting for their orders, they sat quietly. People were passing by in different directions at different speeds and Adam started to think about it. *Where are they going?*

That might seem to be a weird thought, but to him, his next thought was equally peculiar: *Do they know where they are going?* and that thought made him in some way distanced from reality for a second. For some reason, it seemed to him that people did not know, nor were sure where they were going.

Gina noticed his change of mood.

"What's on your mind?" She asked.

He looked at her, but still being in his removed realm he asked:

"Where are they going? Do they know?"

"Who? These people? Oh, I see, you're in your strange philosophical frame of mind now," Gina replied.

"I had a dream last night," started Adam.

Then the waiter showed up with their coffees. Adam seemed to snap out of his strange mood into reality. As the waiter was walking away, Gina picked up the topic, "It seems you've been dreaming quite a bit lately. What was your dream?" She asked.

"What?" Adam answered surprised.

"You said you had a dream. What was it?"

"We were in the St. Peter's Basilica. You know the sculpture of St. Peter, the one that people touch the foot of?"

"Yes, I know."

"So, we were by that sculpture, and you touched it, like everyone else, but then you turned, and you said, you must touch every sculpture there, and you took off, disappearing in the crowd. I only asked if you knew where you were going, but you didn't answer. I tried to follow you, but I couldn't find you," ended Adam.

"And?" Gina asked. "That's it?"

"Then you came from behind me, and you put your arm on me. It seemed kind of heavy touch and the dream was over."

A few seconds passed in silence, and then Gina said, "Then, let's go there."

"Where?"

"There," replied Gina pointing at the St. Peter Basilica dome, clearly visible above the town.

"You know, I thought the same. Let's go there," confirmed Adam.

"Aren't we going to eat anything?"

"Ok, let's get a couple of sandwiches here and we'll be on our way," Adam replied.

They were getting up to get inside when the waiter showed up at the door.

"Can we order a couple of sandwiches to go?" Adam asked.

"Certainly, let me warm them up for you."

Inside the waiter went behind the counter. Adam and Gina looked around. The place was quite small, just a couple of tables.

"Is the ham and cheese all right?" The waiter asked as he pulled sandwiches getting them ready to be warmed.

"One with the ham and cheese, and the other one with just the cheese," said Adam, and Gina nodded. "We pay now for the coffee and sandwiches," he added.

"Yes, of course, two coffees and two sandwiches. Anything else?" The waiter replied.

"No, that's all."

The waiter was collecting payment, when the machine beep announced that the sandwiches were ready. He put them in the bag and presented them to Adam.

"Do you know the quickest way from here to St. Peter Basilica?" Gina turned to the waiter.

"It's quite a distance," he replied. "You'll have to get down the stairs, right there on the corner."

"That's how we got here," Adam interrupted him.

"I see," the waiter continued. "You go down the stairs, then make a right and the street will lead you to the subway station. There you can ask at which station you'll need to get off."

"All right. Thank you," said Gina.

They walked out of the bistro, turned onto the stairs which were still shaded, and walked down.

"And…" started Gina whispering with a fascinated tone in her voice when they entered St. Peter's Basilica.

"And, what?" Adam replied.

"Does it look like in your dream?"

"In my dream?" Adam just recalled an earlier conversation. "No. My dream was about the situation in a certain place, which happened to be this place. No, I have not seen it in my dream," answered Adam equally ravished by the place.

Indeed, they stood in silence at the entrance, enchanted and overwhelmed, looking at the enormous scale and magnificence of the basilica, filled with altars, tombs, sculptures, and paintings. And the mosaic on the floor was endless. Lots of people wondering quietly around were barely noticeable in the vast space of the basilica; stopping at the altars incrusted with elaborate wood decorations; paintings embedded into intricate frames covered with silver and gold; figures sculpted in stone and marble, and expressing pain, joy, suffering, and salvation; saints and blessed looking from above at the passersby. It seemed that this place made people feel like just a tiny addition to the greatness of Christ and His kingdom on Earth. But at the same time, it made faithful people feel as if they already belonged to heaven.

"Should I touch every piece of art here?" Gina joked.

"It's not a dream," replied Adam with a smile.

"But that one, I must touch… You know. St. Peter's," she added.

"It's somewhere in the middle. Let's not rush to it. Let's see the altars on the way."

They passed in silence by marvelous paintings hanging above the altars, lavish decorations around tombs of past, mummified popes, and when they got to the place of St. Peter statue, they stopped. There was a line of people slowly moving toward the sculpture. All wanted to touch the cold stone foot of the Apostol.

There was a short Asian-looking woman in front of them. She must have heard them whispering and she turned a bit to them, trying not to look like she understood the language. As they got close to the statue, she reached out and slid her fingers over the foot of the sculpture. Then Gina and Adam did the same. The woman turned back to them and asked, "Did you touch it?"

Gina and Adam, kind of surprised answered, they did touch it.

"Did you feel it?" The woman asked and without waiting for the answer she said immediately, "It didn't feel like the last time I touched it. I was here two years ago; it was much smoother and felt a lot more delicate under the fingers."

"That's our first time here, we wouldn't know. Sorry," answered Gina still in surprise.

The lady put her head down, turned, and walked away.

Adam and Gina walked around this enormous church for an hour or so, stopping randomly, and taking pictures of statues and paintings. Some of the artifacts were missing and the displayed sign informed that it was taken for the renovation.

They walked out to the sunny and hot afternoon on St. Peter Square and shared mixed feelings about the experience. On the one hand, it was a magnificent place they saw, but the missing sculptures and paintings were a disappointment. They were yearning for more relics and pieces of art.

"What now?" Gina asked.

At that moment, Adam's phone signaled he received an email. He pulled it out.

"Here is your answer," said Adam looking at the phone, and continued, "email from Father Michael."

"Your friend that has a post in the Vatican?" Gina got somewhat excited.

"Yep, our guide," announced Adam.

"What it says in the email?" Gina asked.

Adam scrolled down to the text of the email and started to read aloud, "Sorry for the delay in responding to your email. I'm not in Rome. I was sent on a mission to South America, Brazil's Amazonia and I had no access to the Internet. Now I'm back in Sao Paolo. I will not be back in Rome for some time. But if you need some advice on the Vatican Museum, I suggest you get there early in the morning, at least an hour before the opening, possibly two hours, so you don't stand in the long line to get in."

"Here's our guide..." said Gina unemotionally, when Adam finished reading the email.

"Yeah," answered Adam with some resignation in the tone of his voice.

"How do you know him?" Gina asked.

"I know him from high school. We loosely kept in touch since then. Very intelligent guy, smarter than many kids and very nice at the same time. I was kind of surprised when I learned he went to seminary to be a priest. His parents were from Mexico, so that may explain it. He speaks Spanish perfectly and Portuguese as well. That must be the reason he was sent to South America."

"So, the question remains: What now?" Gina said.

And after a short while, Adam answered calmly and somehow gladly, "Did you really count on him?" and added, "We are on our own. Let's see the art at some other places, other churches."

Then he touched and moved his fingers across his phone's screen looking for the map and directions and said, "Let's see San Pietro in Vincoli. St. Peter in Chains."

"Are we walking? It's hot, you know," said Gina.

"I think we need to take the subway, it's on the other side of the Tiber," said Adam, looking at his phone. "Let's find the closest station."

They passed a couple of blocks and entered a square with an obelisk in the center. A small square formed a kind of large courtyard surrounded by cafés and restaurants with tables and umbrellas. In the center by the obelisk, some kind of gathering began to form as the street performing band mounted their equipment and started to play. And as first tunes of the song came out and spread around the square, Gina said:

"I know this," and stopped as they got halfway to the square.

"That's cool. But let's go. We still have some distance to cover," answered Adam, not really paying attention to the music.

"You said yourself; those places were here a long time before. And they are not going anywhere… Let's have some drinks and listen to the music for a while," replied Gina.

Adam went and ordered drinks at a nearby café and Gina mingled with the small crowd around the band. As he waited for the ordered drinks, music played by the band filled the square and he recognized the song. It was a cover of Joy Division's 'Love Will Tear Us Apart'. When he got the drinks, he noticed that the crowd surrounding the band grew and he lost sight of Gina. Entering the crowd, he spotted Gina on the edge right in front of the performers, so he moved closer to her.

"Here is your drink," he said.

"Thanks," she replied, taking a cup from his hand, still paying attention to the performance.

"You recognized this song even before they really started to play," said Adam.

"Of course, you can't miss it as soon as it starts. I love this song," quickly replied Gina.

***

Walking into the church, initially, they looked at the fresco on the ceiling and passed by the sculpture of Moses. And then driven by curiosity, immediately approached the chamber somewhat lower than the main floor level, where St. Peter's chains were displayed behind the glass case on the altar.

"Do you think they are real?" Gina said quietly.

"Of course, they're real," answered Adam.

As he said that, they noticed a nun kneeling nearby looking at them with a somewhat disapproving look saying that said, "You should be quiet here, at the holy place." That surprised them, as they were only whispering. They

21

sheepishly looked down and walked away to another part of the church.

After some time of walking around the church and appreciating the art installed there throughout the centuries, they stepped out into the hot afternoon and sun-washed square in front of the church. Walking into the nearest shade on the edge of the square, Gina asked again, "Do you think the chains are real? I mean genuine, the actual chains that St. Peter was handcuffed with?"

"No, I don't. They were found and brought here in the fourth century." Saying 'found' Adam made hands gesture symbolizing quotation.

"So, you think they're not genuine?"

"Does it matter to you? It doesn't matter to millions of people. What matters is what they believe. And they believe it is real."

***

A small kid about six or seven years old was moving among the passengers of the subway train. Black, thick, uncombed hair; green pants and a brown hoodie. He was playing harmonica. Or rather it seemed to him that he was playing. He produced a few unordered notes at a time and extended his other hand asking for money from the commuters. Most people ignored him. He stood by Adam and Gina with his trick. As Gina was reaching for a pocket to give him some change, the train stopped and the door behind them opened. Adam touched Gina's arm, "Colosseo, that's our stop. Let's go."

Other people were getting off too, almost forcing both of them out.

A long and steep escalator was taking them up to the street level. As they walked out of the station, across the street ruins of the Colosseum were astonishingly towering in front of them. A feeling of awe overtook them immediately. They looked at each other and smiled as both thought the same—how magnificent this must have been in its glory days, as the mere ruins made such an impression. Walking around the Colosseum they wondered how great it must be inside.

"We don't have time to go inside today," said Gina.

"Yeah, I know. It's going to take at least half a day," answered Adam and added with a hint of resignation in his voice, "We're not going to do it tomorrow. Let's find a place to eat dinner. Then, let's head back to the hotel."

"Right, we need to get up early tomorrow. There are long lines to get to the Vatican Museum," answered Gina.

Walking down the narrow street, packed with gift shops and galleries, they passed a few restaurants and pubs, most of them quite empty. Gina stopped in front of a restaurant with white cloth-covered tables standing on the sidewalk in front of huge, opened windows.

"Let's eat here," she said.

"Sure," answered Adam. "Inside or outside?"

"Inside, let's sit by the window."

They walked in. The place was empty. There was no one there. To Adam, it looked like a perfect place to fulfill his plan. He planned to propose to Gina in Rome, and this quiet, empty, upscale restaurant seemed to be just as he imagined. Well, it wasn't evening yet, the sun was still up, but the place seemed right. They would sit at the white-clothed table, and order good, fresh meals and a bottle of wine. "There will be no candles, but candle dinner seemed such a cliché, and in the evening, the place would probably be crowded," he thought.

They stood in silence for a moment. Then a young girl in a black and white uniform walked up to them.

"Can we sit by the window?" Adam asked pointing to a table.

"Yes, you can sit there," said the girl with a heavy accent.

Her accent was not Italian. It was more like a Russian or Eastern European accent. But neither Gina nor Adam wanted to ask her where she was from. The waitress handed them menus and they walked to the table leaving the waitress behind. Sat down and dove into the menu.

"I'll have chicken pasta," announced Adam.

"I'm going to have pasta, but with shrimp," replied Gina.

"And no sharing," said Adam with a smile.

Then he noticed in the corner of his eye waitress was approaching.

"We'll have pasta, one with chicken and the other with shrimp," he ordered.

"Chicken pasta," repeated the waitress. "I'm sorry. We have no pasta."

"No pasta?" Gina said with real surprise in her voice.

"No pasta in Italy?" Adam added equally surprised.

"We have no pasta at the moment," answered the waitress. "It's early in the evening and pasta is being made fresh right now for tonight. Most of the quest will be coming in an hour or so, and later."

"Oh, so that's why it's so empty here," realized Adam looking at puzzled Gina.

"Yes," said the waitress.

"So, if we come back in an hour, we can have fresh pasta?" Gina asked. "What can we have now?"

"Pizza is always ready," she answered.

Gina looked at Adam and he said, "We'll be back, but for now we'll have pizza. Just cheese pizza."

"Margarita pizza," said the waitress with a smile.

"Yes," replied unsurely Adam and thinking, *Here goes my proposal plan. It would be ridiculous to propose over pizza and beer.*

"So, two margarita pizzas," said the waitress.

"No. Just one pizza," intervened Gina.

"Certainly, one margarita pizza," said the waitress.

Then after a short while, Gina looking at Adam said, "Are we going to come back here later and have fun?"

"Sure, we can," said Adam, "but I thought we have to get up early tomorrow," he added faking a smile and still thinking about the failure of his plan.

***

A weird sound was vibrating in Adam's head. In half-sleep, his eyes closed, he couldn't be sure if it was a reminiscence of last night's escapade to a nightclub or dreams influenced by it, or a combination of both. But as he was waking up, he realized it was a clock alarm buzzing lauder and lauder every second as it seemed. Reaching out to turn off the buzzer, he noticed another sound, the sound of water running in the shower in the bathroom, and realized Gina was already awakened.

"What a night it was," he said when she came out of the bathroom.

"You're still in bed," she replied.

"What a night…" repeated Adam.

"It was your idea."

"My idea?" Adam replied quickly.

"Yeah, you wanted to go back to that restaurant," said Gina.

"But you wanted to go to the club before we even got near that restaurant. It was supposed to be a nice, quiet dinner, but loud music in that club just dragged you in, right? You even liked those gigolos twirling around you on the dance floor," said Adam remembering the last night's events.

"Oh yeah…" continued Gina with a smile, recalling last night's dancing. "And you had fun too, pouring whiskey shots and looking at those girls in tight miniskirts, and high-heels, dancing." And she added, "We can have a nice, quiet dinner when we go to Positano. But now let's go to see the Vatican Museum. It's waiting…"

"Can I take a quick shower?" Adam asked rhetorically.

"Okay, I'll be waiting downstairs in the lobby. Do you want a coffee?" She asked and before Adam could confirm, Gina added, "I'll get you a muffin too."

II

They were approaching the entrance to the Vatican Museum by the wall separating Vatican City from Rome itself. It really looked like the museum was waiting there. But when they got closer, it seemed more like they would have to wait for the museum. Even though it was still early in the morning, the line of people along the wall in front of the entrance was already quite long. People were lining up for a long time before the door of the museum opened.

Most of the people standing in line were quite usual. In a general sense, they were no different from the tourist crowd seen on the streets of Rome. Adam and Gina became part of the queue. And stood, and waited there, so it seemed to Adam as if they melted into a long shape of blurry form of meaningless gooey directed toward the gates of some kind of heaven and waiting for heaven to open. He looked around. Only Gina and a few others, and he, of course, were eager to enter this heaven. Most others were just clueless bystanders wasting time and space, as it seemed to him.

Then the gates to heaven opened.

After they entered, bought tickets, and gathered their guide gear audio player and headphones, they finally entered the first room of the museum. The first thing they heard in the headphones was the announcement saying, "The museum is in the process of major renovation. Most of the items in the exhibitions are undergoing restoration. Some items may be missing from the exhibitions, as noted, or maybe temporarily replaced by the highest quality replicas. Those are noted as well."

Gina and Adam looked at each other somehow puzzled and disappointed and with some kind of resigned agreement. They were hoping to see real pieces of art, but at this point, they had no choice.

"Looks like a big part of heaven is fake," whispered Adam to Gina.

"What?" She asked pulling off her headphones.

"Never mind," answered Adam and they proceeded to encounter real and, as they just learned, not-so-real pieces of art.

They 'walked through', as Gina described the visit to the Raphael Rooms. She was hoping to spend as much time as possible here looking closely, almost examining marvelous sculptures and paintings, but as they learned most of the art in those rooms were copies, she didn't want to really waste her time looking at something that was not original and save the time for the Sistine Chapel.

The crowd poured into the chapel and them with it. Then sudden quietness surrounded them, and they embraced it without hesitation. And then after the moment, the guide's flat voice announced itself yet again, but Gina did not hear it. She pulled off the headphones wire from the guide player, plugged it into her phone, and played her favorite music. This seemed like a ritual for her. Whenever she went to a museum or art gallery, she'd put the headphones on, played the music, and wrapped herself in the art. And it wasn't any kind of music; it had to be one of those long suites of krautrock, German electronic music from the early seventies of the last century.

While the music was building up and settling the mood, Gina was immersed in the Last Judgment painting.

He, the Judge appears glowing on the firmament, coming from the heavens to separate the good from the bad; wheat from chaff. People float, each on their own cloud. Men and women, young and old, naked souls, scarcely covered by the earthly cloths—just the way they were created. Terrified faces; some show anger; and eyes filled with hope; some shy away. Hands are reaching up and hands are reaching down like those a little higher trying in desperation to help and lift those below in resignation. Apathy seals those waiting on the bottom to be judged, reminiscent of any good they could find, but not caring if they will be lifted to heaven. And no hope in clouds for those falling, horrified, gripped by evil, herded, and dragged down to everlasting punishment of hell. The Holy Book faces them and only now, do all realize they were told long before; the judgment and purge were coming.

And as the music was really kicking in now, Gina drifted with them. She could hear them all. Screaming, shouting in distress, and yelling with begging voices. She moved from cloud to cloud looking closely into the petrified faces, wishing eyes and opened mouths releasing songs of glory. Will He like the chorus? Will He be annoyed? Does it matter now? And He seems to be saying, "You kneeled in front of me and said to me—Lord, Lord, and sang to me in churches on Sundays, but it did not occur to you that I could be laying sick and hungry in the street."

Then a sudden clash of thunder changed her attention to the gates of hell. Everything looks backward here. Over the dark waters of the river, she followed them—strong arms of mighty heroes became rounded up, twisted limbs, crippled appendages. The flowing river turned into black lava, holding and pulling in anything that came close to the tentacles of its underground creatures. Voices become sounds of howl bundled into null. And then, the river and all is swiftly taken over by fiery magma, rushing into the underground at a distant point of no return, underneath the mountain.

Adam thought he was ready to move on with the crowd to the next room, but seeing Gina dipped in her world, just stood next to her and knew they could exist in these surroundings for a long time, as he appreciated the art in his own way, on his own level. For him, depictions represent the way people at that time perceived their reality. Events shown on frescos, historically speaking, had never occurred, but for him, art represented consequences of the history teaching, tradition, religion, philosophy, and politics of that time.

After a minute, he decided it was time to move on.

At that moment, Gina felt some disturbance on the fringes of the world she was in. It was a little tap on her shoulder from Adam. Immediately she was pulled into reality. She looked at him as he was giving her signs with his head that it was time to go.

Stepping out of the Sistine Chapel, Gina said to Adam, "Have you noticed missing pieces on the edges of the Last Judgment?"

"Not just the Last Judgment, but other frescos had white spots and missing areas."

"Oh, really?" Gina asked in surprise. "There was not enough time, I only glanced through them and concentrated on the ceiling."

Entering Sobieski Room, Adam whispered, "This is what I wanted to see."

They walked in front of the enormous 30-foot-long and 15-foot-high painting, showing Polish King Jan Sobieski dispatching a letter to the Pope of the victory over the Ottoman siege of Vienna. To Adam, it was a piece of history that occurred a long time ago, but a moment in time that never happened in the way it was portrayed. This was the style of the painter. A conglomerate of different people in different situations, every figure is in one place at the same time, and all take center stage in one layer of the image. No perspective and space dimension, a flat picture with almost no depth except for the background—mountains and the city in the far.

But to Adam, this did not matter much, as the painting was full of symbolic meanings intended by the author. It shows victorious King Jan Sobieski on his horse, appearing to be just coming from the battlefield and stepping over the flag of the conquered vizier. The vizier broke and escaped on his knees through the fields of the atrocities his army committed. At the same time, the king is handing a letter with the victory message to the Pope's courier. Kings of the Holy League and generals of the coalition armies pay their respect and even their horses seem to be bowing to the Polish king. In the background, a legion of famous Polish Winged Hussars, the best and invincible army units of the time are decisively arriving from the mountain with their spears high up and the Holy Spirit hanging above it all. The victory is complete; now the message needs to be sent to the Pope.

This painting tells the whole story of what happened over several days and would take pages of written text to describe. It's preserving history in a very unique way.

"It's reproduction," said Gina quietly.

"How do you know?" Adam asked.

"Colors seem too fresh for the old painting."

"Oh, you're so good at that," applauded Adam.

"No, I just read the note," said Gina with a wicked smile.

Indeed, there was a note below the painting to the left saying, it's the reproduction and the original is being renovated.

Then the passerby speaking to himself, but surely to be noticed, whispered to them with disappointment, "It's the second year I'm coming here to see the original. It's not here. No one knows if it ever is here again."

The hot air of the late afternoon hit them like the heat from opening the oven as they walked out of the cooled museum into the Vatican Gardens. Gina immediately reached out for the water bottle in her backpack and after a few large sips she handed the bottle to Adam saying, "Oh, it's hot here."

Beyond the wall in the short distance, as it seemed, there was the dome of St. Peter Basilica towering over the landscape. A silence of disappointment of a kind surrounded them as they walked the pathways of the garden. Sweaty people were taking selfies in front of sculptures baked by the afternoon sun. Posing to prove and brag they were here and the 'here' meant this place and this time without really comprehending 'where'.

Gina was putting together words in her mind to clearly express her thoughts and feelings and what she was experiencing looking at the paintings, frescos, and sculptures inside. Especially the Last Judgment made lingering impressions. Depiction of despair and repulsion. Inevitable salvation and eradication emanated from the painting.

Then suddenly the silence was torn and injected with the voice coming from the distance. A voice of muezzin calling Muslims to pray.

They look at each other somewhat puzzled. And at that moment, Gina felt that everything she wanted to say was taken away from her.

"I'm sure it's not coming from the basilica," said Adam with a little smile.

"Do you think they will ever pray in St. Peter Square?" Gina asked with a quite serious look.

Still, with the same smile on his face, Adam shook his head and said nothing.

When Muezzin's call for a prayer stopped, Gina said, "I was right about the colors in the painting. I noticed that before I read the note. Some frescos colors also seemed in some parts too fresh and I'm pretty sure, they were also replicas. I think I could do a better job."

"That's disappointing," answered Adam. "I know it means a lot to you and I was hoping you'd get to see originals."

"And I know what those white patches on the edges of some frescos are?" Gina said, as if to herself.

"What are they?" Adam inquired.

"It's a new technology and a trend in renovating ancient art, especially suited for reconstructing wall paintings and sculptures. It was part of my study, and I wrote a paper about it," continued Gina. "Shortly, parts of a painting, in this case, frescos are removed by a tool with laser-guided scanners and special computer software using 3D printing able to recreate that piece exactly. The piece is then placed instead of original, while the original is being renovated with traditional, time-consuming methods."

"Really? That's interesting," said Adam, paused for a second and continued, "so, if it is recreated exactly and replaces the original, that original may never be put back in place and no one would notice."

"Oh, you're right. I never thought of that," said Gina.

"No one, except you," continued Adam with a peculiar face, somehow predicting Gina's next reply.

"We have to go back there," she said, as he had foreseen.

"No, we're not going back to the museum. We have a plan and a schedule, and returning to any place is not in that plan," rebutted Adam. "Today, we still have places to visit. Tomorrow, it's the Ancient Rome tour, almost all day and then we've booked the rental car and we're going to Pompeii and Amalfi."

"I can do it tomorrow," Gina wasn't giving up. "Tomorrow afternoon, I'll visit the Sistine Chapel while you're getting the car and then we can drive down to Pompeii. It's only a couple of hours drive, right? We'll be there before midnight."

"Are you serious? We were going to rent a car together and then go to a nice restaurant for a quiet dinner. You owe me one. Remember?" Adam said, but it didn't sound convincing to Gina.

"You should know by now, what time the nightlife starts here. We can have dinner in the Amalfi in a nice restaurant with a view, somewhere by the sea," replied Gina.

Adam's plan to propose to Gina seemed to fall apart again, or at least needed another alteration.

"First, she dodged a restaurant in Rome, then it was to be Pompeii and now it's Amalfi. She's changing all my plans," thought Adam.

Even though he wasn't entirely sold on the idea, he thought that maybe all these obstacles to his plan happened for a reason. Perhaps it'll be even more romantic to propose somewhere at night on the beach? And that sounded good to him.

"Okay," said Adam reluctantly after a short pause.

Looking at the Colosseum from the outside and exploring its inner architecture was obviously the most impressive of Ancient Rome's fast-paced and intense tour. But in Colosseum, his mind didn't paint gladiators, animals, spelled blood, and silence of the crowd, at the moments when Caesars were deciding the faith of the slaves with the turn of their thumb.

For him, the most memorable was visiting the site of the Circus Maximus. Here, he saw in his mind, riders on horses galloping on the stretches of the sandy tracks and chariots turning sharply around the corners, all breathing heavy in the heat of the day, like today, and all to the noise of the sweaty, yelling crowd. Cheering in excitement or booing in disappointment. It seemed as if he could almost smell it.

But now, dry grass was covering the tracks and center of the field. The seating areas around the stadium were empty and ravaged by the time. As he stood there with his thoughts, the noise of the modern city was floating in quietly. Then on the edge, behind the top of the stadium, over the ancient ruins, in the clear sky, he saw a jet airliner passing high above, like a manifestation of modernity contradicting his visions of this place.

When the tour ended, and before they departed as agreed—Adam to get the rental car, and Gina going back to the Vatican Museum, Adam still was trying to change her mind.

"Are you still going back there?" He asked.

"Back to the museum? Yes," Gina answered sharply.

"Yeah, but we can do it later. You don't have to do it now," Adam was not giving up.

"When?" She asked somewhat irritated.

"When we get back from Amalfi before we fly back. We're still going to be here for the entire day," answered Adam, sensing there might be a chance to convince Gina otherwise.

"Oh, come on. You know, there'll be no time on the day we fly out. Our flight is in the afternoon, and you know how the airports are. We need to be there early. Besides, we talked about it already and we agreed."

That answer destroyed any slightest shade of hope that might have risen moments ago in Adam's mind of convincing Gina to change her plans and just said with an agreeable voice:

"You're taking the subway, right?"

"Yep."

"I'll walk. The rental place is not far from here." He pointed in the direction behind him and continued, "Then I'll drive to the hotel, to get our bags. Where and when we're going to meet?" Adam kept talking, as he wanted to delay the departure.

"You tell me. You'll be driving. Somewhere close to St. Peter's, so I don't have to walk far," said Gina and added, "I'll send you a text."

"Make sure you send me a text when you get to the museum."

They kissed. Gina turned around and started toward the subway station and Adam was watching her walking away. He loved watching her from a distance, as she walked. She knew he was watching. So, just before he moved in his own direction, Gina slowly turned her head at him, looked, and smiled.

Adam

I

Adam was getting into the rental car when his phone alerted him, he a got message. He read with a relief text from Gina, "Just got into the museum. I'll send the next one once done."

So, he drove to the hotel, packed all their bags, then drove near the Vatican walls and started to look for a parking spot. Nothing was available nearby. He navigated small, narrow streets, circling around; looking for any place he could park the car. Although, he wasn't really concerned about unavailability—he had plenty of time, driving around and finding nothing made him kind of impatient and uneasy. When he finally spotted in his rear mirror a car pulling out of the parking spot that he just passed on the side of the street, he stopped, waited a second for the car to pass him, then backed to the place; he parked with some release.

That was further from the Vatican than he thought. Driving around made his sense of the proximity somehow fog. He knew Gina didn't want to walk far, but he could not find anything closer and in his opinion, it was a manageable distance to walk.

As Adam started his stroll toward the Vatican, he checked his phone and saw a message sent by Gina a while ago, unnoticed, when he was occupied with finding a parking spot, which said, "Some weird things are going on here. I'm taking pictures. Tell you later."

The message seemed puzzling. *What kind of things were going on?* He wondered, but he felt relieved that Gina was going to explain it later and assumed she was on her way out of the museum to meet him. He replied, "See you soon in St. Peter Square, at the fountain."

When Adam got to St. Peter Square, the museum was already closed, so he expected Gina to be waiting for him at the fountain. She was not there.

He went to the basilica entrance, thinking that Gina might still be there. But he was told that the basilica was closed to tourists and anyone who was inside had already left.

Adam wandered around St. Peter Square, sending desperate messages to Gina's phone to no avail. He even didn't realize when it got dark, and the fountain got lit up with colors. But for him, as in a bad dream, visions of what could happen to her were spinning around his mind, as he pushed them off with one hope that, like a couple of days ago in the airport, Gina would show up right behind him saying, "I'm here."

That didn't happen. It was getting late. The thoughts of what could happen to Gina were coming back and intensifying. He was imagining her being dragged off the street by a sex-hungry teenage group of thugs and raping her. Or being snatched by hoodlums kidnapping young girls and selling them to the mafia as a sex slave for the rich Arabs.

Then Adam finally pushed away all the dreadful thoughts and put himself into rational mode. He walked out of the St. Peter Square looking for the police.

At the police station, he talked about his situation to the officer. The officer took some notes and in broken English told him to come back tomorrow when there was going to be someone who spoke English and would properly file the case.

On the way to the car, he phoned the U.S. Embassy in Rome, but it was already closed, so he only left a voice message.

He thought about finding a hotel, but eventually ended up slipping in the car.

The next day from the moment that he woke up, all that he was doing, even though real, seemed like a bad dream and that at some point he'd wake up. He was the engine behind all of the things that were happening around him, but it didn't feel like he was part of the process. He was zoned out. Everything was going on beyond the transparent wall or a cocoon surrounding him.

In the morning when he returned to the police station, they took all the information, filed the case and he was told to report the missing person to the Vatican Gendarmerie, as per his statement, Gina entered Vatican City before the disappearance.

Adam decided to go to the U.S. Embassy first because he hadn't received a reply to his message. He drove in traffic across the city, and then at the embassy's security check, he showed two passports, his and Gina's, and explained his situation. Then he was directed to an appropriate office in the building and waited, and waited, and waited, and finally, the door to the office opened and he was invited to come in. There he repeated all the events again. The person he spoke to, took his contact information, expressed concerns, and declared to stay on top of the case. Then he was advised to visit the U.S. Embassy in the Vatican, called the U.S. Embassy to the Holy See, which was just a block away, and report his case there.

So, he went there and the same humdrum of telling his story went on again.

He talked about visiting St. Peter's Basilica, taking a tour of the museum, Vatican Gardens, and so on, and Gina wanting to go back to the museum. Then as previously, he was told to report his case at the Vatican Gendarmerie and was given the address to the proper office.

When he arrived after yet again, a long drive in the city traffic, all seemed to follow the same routine as in previous places: he was directed to wait in front of the office, then asked to enter and report what happened.

He didn't realize it at the time, but here they already knew about his case and waited for him. So, here again, he told his story to the gentleman sitting behind the desk. He said they separated and that was the last time he saw Gina. He went to get a car and Gina went to the Vatican. They were going to meet in St. Peter's Square in the early evening, but she did not come.

"Did you receive any messages from Gina after you separated?" He was asked.

"Messages?" Adam asked with a surprise.

"Did she call you or send you any messages?"

That question was like a wake-up call that pulled him out of the lethargy that he seemed to feel all day. Reality came into focus now. *How did they know, she even had a phone on her? I never told anyone that she contacted me when she got into the museum*, he thought.

"Did you or did you not? Are you telling everything you know?" He was asked again.

At that moment, Adam felt like he was being interrogated. Maybe they need more information from him to conduct the investigation.

"Yes, Gina sent me a text that she is in the museum."

But his doubts about the situation did not leave him, so he decided not to reveal anything about the second text Gina sent him later.

"Is that all? That's all you received from her?"

That was confirmation of his suspicion that they were not telling him all they knew.

"Yes," answered Adam.

"In that case, I don't have any questions. Do you?" The gentleman asked.

"What are the next steps? What are you going to do?"

"Well, in a couple of minutes, we'll receive the printed version of your statement, which is made from the recording of this conversation, and you will be free to go."

"What about Gina?" Adam asked anxiously.

"We don't know; the investigation has just begun. We'll keep you informed," answered the gentleman and added unfeelingly, "are you going back to the United States soon?"

"I'm not going anywhere until Gina is found," said Adam decisively, feeling like they were trying to get rid of him.

"As you wish," was the cold answer.

Silence filled the room for a moment, and Adam thought to himself, *So, they're recording it all without asking me first*. Then the silence was broken by the buzzing sound of the printer. Adam was handed a couple of pages, read through it, and after signing his statement, he was escorted outside of the building.

As he walked a couple of blocks to his car, he felt like he was being watched. He became suspicious of several men he spotted behind, or in front, crossing the street, or just standing on the corner that he thought were watching him. Maybe it was just the illusion or the impression filling his mind, which was a product of him not saying anything about the second message from Gina and them not telling all they seemed to know.

Adam got into his car, shut the door, and looked around for anyone that might resemble in any way the men he thought, were following him. But no one was there. No one was looking at him. People were passing by on the sidewalks on both sides of the street not paying attention to him at all. Why would anyone be interested in him? Then he thought he was getting paranoid about the situation… His thoughts just mingled around Gina's disappearance, and as he viewed it, his interrogation at the Vatican Gendarmerie. That lasted for some time, but in the end, he concluded that no one would really care or was even interested in him. And that thought that nobody cared, and the suspicion he developed at the gendarmerie's office, lingered.

Adam got out of his car with ideas spinning in his mind and he put them into the plan of action.

He walked less than half of the block, entered a small hotel, and asked for a single room. He stepped into the room and looked around. The room was tiny, but that didn't matter. He didn't care about it. His mind was occupied with the plan of finding Gina. And the main point of this plan at the moment was Gina's phone.

Adam thought of his friend whom he had not spoken to in a while. They were not really friends, but a few years ago, they had a good relationship. Nick was his name. Nick was a computer-network-internet geek. At that time, most of the people steered away from him as much as he kept away from them. He was a weirdo in some sense, even Adam thought that. But in an odd way, he was nice, cool, and approachable as long as he was interacting with others out of his own will and not being made or forced to do it.

Maybe Nick could locate Gina's phone and that could be the starting point for Adam's own independent way of finding her.

Later he found Nick's number on his phone. He knew it was an old number, but entered text to send, "Hi Nick, this is Adam. I hope you remember me. I'm in Rome. This is an unusual situation, I'm in dire straits. Please text me back or call me. I need your help."

Soon after, the reply came in, "Message was not delivered. This number is not in service."

II

Lying on the small bed in the tiny room, Adam saw his plan did not even really launch and failed at the start, or at best got very complicated with the very first step. He then realized he did not have a real plan. What would he do if he located Gina's phone? Go to that unknown location, which could be far or even dangerous. Or maybe let the police know? But the experience he already had with the police told him it could take a day or two before any action would take place. He didn't have a plan. He just needed to know where she was.

Then his phone rang. He looked up at the display, and the number was not recognized. A few thoughts crossed his mind. It was too late for the embassy to call; it was already closed. Maybe the police? But his adrenaline rushed, and he got scared when he thought it could be a call from the kidnappers that he imagined earlier.

"Yes?" He said answering the call.

"Hi, Adam. This is Nick. I got your message."

At that moment, some relief descended over Adam, as he heard Nick's voice. Even though he hadn't heard it for some time, he thought he recognized it.

"Hi," said Adam somewhat excited. And as soon as he said that, unexpectedly some doubts and suspicious feelings entered his thoughts, like that one-off being followed, when he left the Vatican Gendarmerie: *How did he get my message if his number was not in service? Is this really Nick?*

"Of course, I remember you," continued Nick. "In school, you seemed to me to be on the fringes of any social involvement. Obviously, not like myself, totally aloof and antisocial type, but I liked about you that distant friendliness."

That kind of surprised Adam, he never thought of himself that way, being distant-friendly. Well, that must be Nick; he was and still is weird. That made Adam relax and forget about his suspicions, but still, he asked, "How did you get my message? The replay said the number is not in service."

"I know. It's my older number, but I keep it and that message is generated if I don't pick up the phone. And I don't pick up the phone if I don't know who is calling."

"Can you help me? I'm in Rome," said Adam. "And my girlfriend disappeared, here in Rome."

"This is serious shit, man," interrupted Nick.

"Really? No shit," answered Adam thinking Nick was referring to his message and feeling he got Nick's attention to the proper level of urgency.

"Your phone communication and location are being traced as we speak."

"That's why I contacted you in the first place, to trace and find my girlfriend's phone. But who is tracing me?"

"I don't know, but I see, monitoring of your phone started yesterday," replied Nick.

"Why? By whom?" Adam kept asking.

"I said, I don't know."

"But whoever they are, they know I'm talking to you," stated Adam.

"Oh, no," quickly replied Nick. "I have implemented precautionary measures. I sent them on a goose chase around the planet. When you called my old number, they thought you called someone in Tokyo. I called you from Montevideo, Uruguay, and by now, they think you speak to somebody in Johannesburg, South Africa."

"But they can be listening and even recording our conversation," said Adam.

"They might, they probably are, but it's all scrambled and useless noise to them. I told you; I took precautionary measures," answered Nick with some satisfaction in his voice and added, "you get yourself a new SIM card, pull out the one that's in your phone, and insert the new one. Better yet, get yourself a new phone with a European SIM and still pull the old SIM from your old phone, as they could trace your location that way. Then, send me a text at the same number. Got it?" Nick finished with the question.

"Sure, got it," said Adam quickly just as the call disconnected.

Adam went out to get a new phone. As he walked for a couple of blocks looking for a store selling phones and SIMs, he again got this strange feeling of being followed. But as recalled what Nick said about his phone being traced, he realized that was unlikely. Whoever they were, they didn't have to follow him, and they knew where he was by his phone position. That realization gave him an idea.

He walked down the stairs to the subway station nearby. After buying a one-way ticket and waiting for a few minutes, he got on the train. He then took an empty seat in the corner. Everybody else was mining their own business with their faces glued to their phones. Adam slowly dropped his phone to the floor and pushed it underneath the seat. He got off at the next station and walked back to his hotel. On the way, he stopped at a store and bought a new phone with a prepaid card.

At the hotel, he sent a message to Nick with his girlfriend's phone number, and then he paid for his last night's stay, got into his car, and drove away not sure where he was heading.

***

Adam drove for some time and left the city, entering a rural area. He exited the highway and drove on a small countryside road, shaded by the trees. Passing white and pink villas visible in the distance on a hill surrounded by orchards, he thought how wonderful it would have been if Gina was here with him.

Then the sudden buzz of his phone pulled him out of his dreamlike thoughts. The phone messenger was showing a call from Helsinki. Adam picked it up figuring it was Nick and said, "Hi."

"Hey," answered Nick on the other side. "You've got a new phone. Good. Did you pull the SIM card from the old one?"

"No," said Adam. "I kept the phone turned on and left it on the subway train. Let them trace that," he added.

"Excellent," replied Nick and continued, "I see you're not in Rome."

"No. I left the hotel and drove outside the city."

"Listen, you have to go back there. Your girlfriend is in Rome."

"What? She's there? Where?" Adam jumped, pulling to the side.

"Well, I traced the last signal of her phone to Vatican City. To be precise, to the building on Via del Pellegrino. It's headquarters of Vatican police."

"I know, I was there yesterday," replied Adam with excitement. "I'm going back."

"Hey Adam, what was the last message you got from Gina?" Nick asked.

"She texted me; she was taking some interesting pictures on her phone."

"When was that? Do you remember?"

"Late, late afternoon," replied Adam.

"Before 8 p.m., you think?" Nick kept asking.

"Oh, I'm sure it was before 8," was Adam's answer.

"The last transmission from that phone was a couple of minutes after 9 p.m. It looks like a large amount of data was sent," continued Nick. "I don't know what was sent or where, but I'll keep digging."

"Nick, you have no idea, how much I appreciate your help with this," said Adam.

"No sweat, man, you know me, I like that stuff. I'm the weird one," said Nick and added, "you just make sure you find your girl."

Driving back to the city, Adam was excited that Gina was alive, but then again, got him into the thinking mood, as Nick's words were still buzzing in his head, "You just make sure you find your girl."

The weird one, the outsider, almost rejected one put a positive current in him, injected motivation, and gave him hope. Yet again, his mind was not satisfied.

I found my girl already. She just disappeared and left me suddenly. Maybe she left me of her own will? He kept thinking.

Once that thought emerged in his mind, he asked himself what the reason was. What was the reason for her to be with him in the first place? And he concluded it was love. What could be more important for her than love? But then, he kept drilling the subject and asked himself, was he the only love for Gina? And he did not have any other person in mind; he meant love in general, a love that could be more important for her than he.

"I'm just going nuts," said Adam out loud, realizing no one listened and no one would care.

And he had a task at hand.

As he was getting closer to the city, he got his phone and dialed the Vatican police.

"This is Adam Ross," he said when some woman on the other end picked up the phone and said something in Italian, which Adam thought was a customary answer "How can I help you?"

"Do you speak English?" and didn't wait for the answer. "I was in your office yesterday and I spoke with Officer Cornellio. Can you transfer me to him?"

Then after a second, he heard the same voice speaking in English:

"Please wait."

"Mr. Ross, I'm glad you called. Where are you?" Adam heard Cornellio's voice.

"Hi. I'd like to meet with you. I have the information… It'll help to find Gina. I need to meet with you," rushed Adam.

"What information?" Cornellio asked. "Tell me now."

For some reason, Adam felt uncomfortable telling over the phone what he had learned about Gina's phone, he replied:

"The information I have, I can only deliver in person. Can we meet today? It's important."

"Of course, I understand, it's important. I will be waiting in my office for the rest of the day," answered Cornellio.

Driving toward the city, Adam thought of ways of approaching the situation, which meant confronting Cornellio with the facts he did not disclose but must have known—as Adam assumed. *Obviously, I must tell him, I traced the phone, but should I ask him in a polite way, why he didn't tell me Gina was there? Or ask the questions in a firm and strong way. Or maybe not ask him, but just burst into his office and demand answers. What are they hiding from me?*

His thoughts were interrupted when the phone buzzed. Adam looked at the lit-up screen. It showed a call was coming from Vladivostok. He picked it up.

"Hey Nick, what's up?" He said.

"Hey. You tell me what's up. Your new phone is being traced now. Whom did you call from that phone?"

"Just you and the Vatican police to let them know, I'm coming," answered Adam taken by surprise.

"Now we know who is following you," said Nick and continued, "listen, that last transmission from Gina's phone with a ton of data… She sent lots of images to her cloud storage."

"Yeah, she said in her text, she was taking pictures," replied Adam. "Can you get those pictures?"

"Already did," quickly said Nick.

"What's on them?" Adam kept asking.

"I don't know, didn't look at them," and he changed the subject then. "So now, you're going back there?"

"Yeah, we need to end this call," Adam cut him off, as he was in the city and wanted to concentrate on driving and navigating the streets.

"Be careful, it seems like you stepped into some serious shit," replied Nick and ended the call.

Adam parked the car a block away from the Vatican police building, the closest available spot. Sat in the car gathering his thoughts and strategizing the approach of the discussion with Cornellio. He felt Cornellio wasn't honest or wasn't telling all he knew. That feeling grew, when he recalled, who might trace his phone. Nick's words 'serious shit' was buzzing in his head, as he was trying to comprehend the situation. "What shit? How serious? What's going on?"

But now he needed to concentrate on something else. *I ask him why they're tracing my phone. But he can deny any knowledge and I don't have proof. So, maybe it's not a good idea to even mention it?* He thought. *I'm going to confront him about Gina. Yes, that's most important: ask about Gina. I'll just ask him why she's being held there and demand to see her and then release her.*

When Adam entered the building, walked up the stairs, and passed the secretary, as she was showing him the way to enter Cornellio's office, he was energized to demand answers but was not prepared for what was in store.

"Mr. Ross, please sit down," said Cornellio and the secretary closed the door behind Adam.

"My fiancé is here," surged Adam and continued his burst. "Why didn't you tell me that yesterday? I've been able to trace her phone to this location. You should know about cell phone tracing," he said and regretted it right then, as he felt, he said too much.

He did not expect his level of energy to be deflated so easily and so quickly when Cornellio answered, "Your fiancé is not here; I can assure you of that." And after a short pause, he said, "We tried to contact you, but you were not answering the calls."

There Adam realized, they were calling the phone he dropped in the subway, and that made him feel foolish, as he didn't think at the time that someone may want to call him, so he just said, "I lost my phone."

"Let me explain," followed Cornellio. "This morning came the report to our office from the Vatican Museums' security. It stated that on the previous day, they apprehended Ms. Gina Nolan after she breached the museum's policies and entered areas off limits to the museum visitors. At the same time, we received the package with the phone from security, which was found in the ladies' room, in the museum. We checked the connections made from that phone, and several were made to your phone." Cornellio paused for a second again and then continued, "We have your report, we have the security report, and we have the phone." Then he showed Adam Gina's phone and asked, "Is this your fiancé's phone?"

"Yes, it is," answered Adam recognizing Gina's phone.

Even though all that Cornellio said was logical, seemed to make sense, and was convincing, Adam still felt suspicious, as all of it did not answer his question, which he voiced out, "Where is Gina?"

"I told you, she's not here. The report indicates she was questioned by security and then let go. She left the museum. We have video from our security camera installed by the entrance to the museum, showing her leaving."

Cornellio put a stick drive into his laptop and played the recording, "Please take a look."

Adam stepped closer to the desk and looked at the screen. The video showed Gina walking out through the swing door at the museum entrance.

"Can you identify her? Is this Ms. Gina Nolan, your fiancée?" Cornellio asked.

After a short glimpse of the girl's face on the video, Adam had no doubts. "Yes, this is Gina," he answered. Shocked and shattered he asked, "Can I get this video?"

"I cannot give it to you," quickly answered Cornellio and added, "because you filed a missing U.S. citizen with the U.S. Vatican Embassy, I will send this report and the video attached to it, to the embassy. The phone will also be sent there. Then you'll need to talk to them, they will help you."

Walking out of Cornellio's office, Adam called the U.S. Embassy, referred the situation, and asked for a meeting the next day. He was told he would be contacted once the report arrived and then should arrange the meeting. Believing the report would be there tomorrow; he begged to set up a meeting the next day afternoon and hoped it would arrive on time.

Then he wandered around Rome, along the ancient ruins, and tiny streets, climbing stairs, passing squares decorated with fountains or statues in the center, but really going nowhere. But he didn't care about the beautiful, narrow streets, windows filled with flowers, or smiling people, sitting in the shade outside of the cafes. He didn't care, even when he entered, obviously unplanned the small square where Gina and he stopped the other day to listen to the street playing band. Now there was a lonely man singing Pink Floyd's 'Another Brick in the Wall'. Adam moved on, to nowhere.

Only two things were on his mind as he was walking oblivious around Rome. Will he get into the embassy tomorrow? And if he will, will he get a copy of the police report and most importantly, the video of Gina?

And there was the other thing on his mind, which seemed to be always sitting somewhere in the back of his head since Gina's disappearance, and he was pushing it away every time it surfaced. But since this morning, against all his will, it began to take more and more center stage of his thoughts. He had to contact Gina's parents and tell them what happened.

Guilt was the term and the reason for which he was trying to avoid that thought. But in reality, he knew it was just a layoff.

56

III

The plane was already over the Atlantic and Adam was leaning back in the seat with his eyes closed. He was not asleep.

Yesterday he met with embassy officials, and received copies of all reports, Gina's phone, and the video of her leaving the museum. He was persuaded to go back to the United States, as his case was put through the police and security systems and there was nothing more, he could do there. He was assured that he would be contacted immediately, as soon as new information about Gina surfaced or if anything changed in this case. So, he arranged to get on the first available plane from Rome to Chicago.

He understood the reality of the situation and he had to admit to himself that his presence wasn't changing anything, and even though he tried to oppose it in his mind, his resistance was futile. But at the same time, the guilt he felt was not leaving him.

Before he got on the plane, he called Gina's parents. No one answered and he was directed to the voicemail. In his message, he said he was returning to the States, but Gina was not with him, and that he would explain the situation when they met after his return. He felt some kind of relief that he did not speak with them directly, but he knew it was only postponing the moment when he would have to face them.

His eyes were still closed, and his thoughts were vying through his mind. He blamed himself for what happened. "If only, I didn't let her go there that day? But how couldn't I? She was so convincing in persuading me. Or was she? No, it was I that was so easily convinced. I should have stopped her."

He dwelled on the guilt that was subsiding and then again intensifying with each and every thought. *I let her go. I'm coming home and I left her there. She's mine and I left her and abandoned her. I let her go. I am a coward. How could I do that? But then again, what else could I do? I had nothing to hang on to.*

He was battling with his thoughts and then it came—the urge to see Gina.

He set up, picked up his tablet, where he loaded the video of Gina walking out of the museum and started to watch. The video was less than thirty seconds long, so he turned on continuous play and watched it again, and again, and again. As he watched it, he saw Gina inside the museum walking up to the revolving door, moving through it to the outside, and then walking away.

As he watched it again and again, he was focused on Gina's face. Then, for some reason, he turned his attention to the other aspects of the situation recorded in the video. Walking toward the door, Gina was looking at the phone; she turned to the swinging door and walked through. Then outside after a few steps, she looked at the phone again.

Further away in the frame beyond her, he could see a street leading uphill and a clear, bright sky beyond in the distance.

Then it struck him. "The sky… It's daylight. But the last she used the phone was after 9 at night." He realized the footage he got must have been taken earlier, before 9 p.m., as it wasn't dark outside. That meant Gina walked out of the museum and then she returned, as her phone was found inside the museum. It was puzzling and he tried to make sense out of it.

It felt really weird. At first, he felt angry that he was duped and easily dismissed by the Vatican police with just a few seconds of the video. As he admitted to that fact, there was obviously more to it than he previously thought. And then he recalled Nick's words, "You stepped into some deep shit." At the same time, being unwillingly involved in something conventionally unexplainable, he felt rejuvenated, motivated, and even excited to do something, and that something was obviously to continue to look for Gina.

Realizing that proper and institutional means of achieving his goal were at least questionable or perhaps those institutions—police, gendarmerie, and embassies were even negatively involved in it, Adam thought of his own, independent pursuit of the case. Puzzling for him was—why would they be involved that way? And he kept repeating to himself, "Think, think. You're on your own and no one else is there."

He opened his eyes. The drinks were being served.

Was he sleeping? Dreaming? Gina walking out? Empty street. Blue sky in the distance. Police hiding facts and even covering up.

The tablet in front of him was in sleep mode—black screen. He knew he watched that video of Gina, but he was not sure if his thoughts were real or just a mishmash of reality and dreams. He started the tablet video to make sure it wasn't a dream. He looked at the video again and paid special attention to the sky visible beyond. Now Adam was sure, it was not a dream; it was daylight when Gina walked out of the museum.

As soon as the plane landed, he tried to send the text to Nick, eager to share his video discovery and hoping Nick would help him in solving this situation, but his 'European' phone would not connect to any network. *Damn phones,* thought Adam, walking out of the customs. He looked around and went straight to the nearest public phone. He inserted the card and dialed Nick's phone, but there was no answer. No answer at all. The dial signal was buzzing vainly in his ear for a long time—no answer, no connection, nothing. He wouldn't even get to the voice mail. "Yeah, he's not going to pick it up."—Adam hung up, assuming it was one of Nick's strange precautionary measures, as he was calling from the public phone.

On the way home, Adam stopped at the shop of his cell phone provider. Explained he had lost his phone in Europe and now he got a new phone with a new number. Stepping out of the store he sent a text to Nick, simply stating, "This is Adam. We need to meet."

Soon after, he got the reply, "When and where?"

"Tonight, the cross-eyed dudes," was Adam's answer.

"Where is that?" Nick was asking.

"Joe Manhattan's Bar," texted surprised Adam.

The Joe Manhattan's Bar was the place they called 'the cross-eyed dudes' back in school days. It was near the school. The owner was crossed-eyed and that's where the name of the place came from. They hung out there sometimes and Adam was sure Nick must have been there and must have known the place.

"See you there tonight," a message from Nick displayed on Adam's phone.

Adam was walking down the sidewalk in the old neighborhood and approaching Joe's Bar. He hasn't been to this area for some time. He picked up this place to meet with Nick almost unconsciously, as back then they all hung around here.

Then, some suspicious thoughts came in. *How come Nick seemed not to know the cross-eyed dudes? Maybe it wasn't Nick I was exchanging messages with?* He realized he actually hadn't spoken with Nick since before the visit to the Vatican police and since then he had yet another phone. And as he wasn't sure now whom he was in contact with, he got kind of scared. He looked around nervously, but no one was following him or even paying attention to him. Then, suddenly, out of nowhere, light rain started to cover the street and Adam hurried up to the 'cross-eyed dudes'.

It was still early evening and not too many people were inside. Adam sat at the corner of the bar, watching the entrance, drinking beer, pushing away those weird, suspicious thoughts that someone else might show up instead of Nick, and replacing those feelings with convictions that Nick would be here soon.

Two guys set by the counter drinking and watching a game on the TV screen hanging above. It was not possible for Adam to watch the game on the crooked screen from this angle. It was hard to even recognize the game, as most of the time no one was moving on the screen. It could have been baseball or golf.

Across the room, two guys and a girl were playing the pool. The submissive balls in the green sky were rolling in many directions, bouncing off the edges, as well as other balls, continuing across the galaxy, sometimes almost touching the fringes of the black hole, and sometimes falling into the abyss. This created smiles on their faces.

The beer glass gradually emptied, but before that happened it was replaced with the full one by the wag of the finger.

Relaxed and somehow hypnotized by watching the pool game, Adam forgot about the entrance and suddenly, some tall, but skinny figure stood by him and sat on a chair next to him, and he immediately recognized Nick.

"Hi, Adam," said Nick, taking off his wet glasses, and reaching for the napkin, wiped his bonny face off the rain drops falling from his wet, thin hair, then started to clean his glasses. "It's been a few years, but I recognized you right away."

"Hi, Nick, I'm glad to see you," answered Adam.

Now Nick seemed a bit skinnier than a guy Adam kept in his memory. Maybe it was just a distortion of the memory caused by the passage of time. It's been several years since he last saw Nick. Or maybe it was just an impression caused by his wet clothes and hair.

"I see it's still raining," said Adam. "What are you drinking?" He added.

"Yeah, it's raining now," answered Nick in disappointment. "How are you?" He asked.

"I don't know. I don't know where Gina is. I need help," answered Adam with resignation.

"I'll have whatever Pils you have on tap," said Nick to the bartender, and turned to Adam. "How can I help?"

"Do you have those images Gina took that day and transferred to the cloud?"

"Yeah, but not with me."

"That's fine. You said they were transferred after 9 p.m., right?" Adam kept asking.

"I think so," said Nick quickly. "I can check."

"The Vatican police told me, Gina was apprehended by the museum security, supposedly for entering restricted areas. Then she was questioned and then released. And they showed me the video from the monitoring system, showing her walking out of the museum."

"Do you have that video?" Nick asked with interest.

"Yes. They gave me a copy. There is something odd about it and that's what I want to talk to you about."

"Okay, let's see it."

"I have a memory stick," said Adam.

"Fine, let's go to my place," answered Nick with excitement. "It's not far."

It was dark and the rain stopped before Adam and Nick arrived at his apartment. They walked into the building and Nick led him to the semi-basement and then entered quite a large room somewhat separated into several areas. The main 'room' had a couch in front of the huge screen. To the left was the area that looked like a kitchen with a breakfast bar opened to the main room. On the counter were empty cups, beer bottles, and boxes of Chinese leftovers. To the right, several shelves set in a U-shape reaching almost to the ceiling encompassed all kinds of computers, switches, cables running from one box to another, multicolor lights blinking, and several screens around one, big one at the 'center' of the 'U'. It appeared to Adam as one huge machine supporting some kind of life.

"You rent this place?" Adam asked.

"Sort of," said Nick and continued, "my folks own this building and rent apartments. At some point, I wanted to move out of the house, so they gave me this basement. I don't pay rent, but it was empty and naked if you know what I mean. I fixed it up the way you see it, made it into a livable place," and added with a smile, "you see, I don't require much."

"Cool," replied Adam.

"Let's see what you've got," said Nick sitting down in front of the big screen of his 'life support machine'.

Adam handed him the memory stick with video, which Nick plugged into one of the computers. Then he touched some icons on the screen, the video started to play, and Adam began explaining the observation he made:

"You see, Gina is walking out of the museum."

"Yeah, what's odd about it?" Nick asked.

"Look at the sky in the background," cut quickly Adam. "It's daylight."

"You're right, but I still don't get it. What's so unusual about it?" Nick said.

"You said Gina transferred those images around 9 p.m., right? It was dark by then," Adam kept explaining.

"So, what? She could send them to the cloud from anywhere," and with quick apprehension, he added right away, "so, how come they got her phone?"

"Exactly," jumped Adam. "I'm sure she was inside the museum when she sent them," said Adam with some kind of satisfaction and continued, "if she'd walked out with the phone and then a few hours later she transferred images, how come they've got the phone? They told me, they found it in the ladies' room, inside the museum. But, if she left the museum without the phone, who sent those images to her cloud account later? And there is one more thing, Gina sent me a text, saying she's inside and something weird is going on there, and that she's taking pictures. That was before 8 p.m. that day. I never told that to anyone."

"Oh man, you're right. Oh man, I knew you stepped into some serious shit," said Nick breaking a short while of silence.

"What you mean, serious shit? They lied to me," said Adam with little anger.

"That's what I mean. It must be serious, and it looks like some kind of cover-up," answered Nick.

"Cover-up of her disappearance? Where is Gina? What happened to her?" Adam kept asking.

"Let's see those pictures she took," said Nick, turned to the monitor, touched some icons, and brought up the first image to the screen.

At first, they couldn't make up anything of the image, it was a bit fuzzy, and it looked like a close-up of a bright, pale face. The next image was the same, but sharper and they noticed tiny black, shiny dots on the face, which by now they realized was a sculpture. Flipping through the images showing figures from different angles, they saw all of them had little, glossy dots, and those specks were not randomly placed. The placement of them seemed to show some kind of a designed pattern. One of the images displayed a kind of bluish beam hitting the sculpture, but they had no idea what it was. Maybe it was a glitch in the picture caused by a strange reflection of the light. Maybe a distortion of the digital data during the process of image saving or during the image upload.

They've been flicking through the images back and forth for some time.

"What do you think?" Nick said. "I can't make anything out of it."

"Neither do I," replied Adam.

"They must be important or at least mean something if she transferred them to the cloud," said Nick and added, "she didn't upload anything else."

"I know what it is," replied Adam. "Gina told me about this new technology to preserve and restore art. She was into it in her study. It involves laser 3D scanning of artifacts and 3D printing, which basically is recreating the piece of art. I can get in touch with her professor and confirm that."

"Interesting," said Nick. "Sure, you can talk to the professor, but what it's got to do with Gina's disappearance?"

"I don't know, man. I don't know," said Adam with tiredness in his voice and added, "but it must be important. You said it yourself."

"So, what are you going to do?" Nick asked, getting up and walking toward the kitchen area. "Do you want a beer?"

"Yeah, beer would be fine," replied Adam and added, "I've got a tough day tomorrow."

"Are you going to contact that professor?"

"Yes, but first I'm going to talk to Gina's parents," answered Adam with the same tiredness in his voice.

***

Heavy fog lingered over the city's gray morning when Adam woke up and looked outside from his bedroom window. Before he opened his eyes and got up, just for one brief moment, he thought that meeting with Nick, on-screen images, Gina's disappearance, and everything around it, could be just a dream. But that lasted less than a second. Then for a short while he imagined it was the day, they were flying to Italy. He'd get up, shower, and go to the airport where he'd meet with Gina, and everything else would just go as planned. But he knew it wasn't the same day and what happened, happened for real. And now when he got up, the feeling of guilt appeared and grew, quickly taking over his thoughts. That feeling increased even more when he picked up his phone, recalling that last night he sent a message with his new phone number to Gina's parents, and now he saw missed calls. He knew that the voicemail icon surely indicated a message from them.

Adam made a call. He asked if they could meet around noon, and he would explain everything. As soon as he was invited for lunch, he made sure to quickly end the call and not to get into any conversation. It may seem like another relieving delay for him, but in his own mind, he knew, he ran out of time, and now, very soon he will have to explain and apologize for what happened.

Approaching Nolan's house, he was mentally preparing himself for an attack. A barrage of questions, misunderstandings, and allegations implied he did not take enough care, neglected the situation and finally in effect, abandoned Gina.

The door opened quickly after Adam pressed the doorbell button. Mrs. Ellen Nolan, Gina's mother appeared. This time as always, elegant and behaved with manners.

"Adam, come in," she said quite nicely, which surprised Adam not expecting this kind of welcome.

"Mrs. Nolan, I'm sorry," started Adam.

"Adam, come in," she repeated interrupting him, but he sensed a deep concern.

The calmness in her voice and peace expressed on her face eased Adam's anxiety in some way, as he was walking to the living room, but that feeling vanished as quickly as it came in, when Gina's father, Brian Nolan appeared stepping down the stairs. He was a tall man. He seemed kind of rugged on the outside with his frankness, which was coming from his intelligence, but nevertheless kind and warm on the inside, which he for some reason was not reviling.

"Adam, how are you? Have a seat," said Mr. Nolan unemotionally.

It definitely didn't sound quite as warm as the welcome from Ellen, which put Adam into the previous state of thought and reminded him that he had expected some kind of cold reception.

As Adam set down on the couch, as close to the edge of it as possible, Brian Nolan asked a simple question, but in a rhetorical manner, "Adam, where is our daughter?"

For a second, Adam tried to put together an explanation, but the question was so direct, that he only came up with, "I don't know."

Brian made a couple of steps and set down on the chair facing Adam and obviously ignoring his answer, said:

"You and Gina went together on a trip to Italy. You came back, but she did not. We have received your calls and your messages that she's not coming back with you."

"Mr. Nolan, let me explain," jumped Adam, but he was interrupted.

"We were also contacted by the U.S. Embassy in Rome. Are you going to explain Gina's disappearance?" Brian said in an attacking voice.

"No, I can't explain that," said Adam and added, "and I don't know where Gina is."

Mrs. Nolan sitting on the opposite end of the sofa entered the conversation calmly, but firmly turning to Adam, "We are terrified. Tell us what happened."

It seemed for a moment like he was going to repeat the same story he told the police and at the embassy. But he realized, it was a very private conversation, and this time he started differently, "I was going to propose to Gina on this trip. Here is the ring," said Adam, pulled the diamond ring from his pocket, and handed it to Mrs. Nolan.

Then he continued telling the sequence of events with all the details he could recall. Described how Gina was fascinated by the art in the museum, and intrigued by the restoration processes, and that curiosity transformed into suspicions, and how she decided to return there, against Adam's reasoning and pleads. Then talked about his doubts about the Vatican police, but he kept details to himself and did not mention Nick's name and his involvement. In the end, Adam felt helpless, and his feelings seemed to spread around the room.

Silence lay unbearably heavy.

Listening to the story, Brian Nolan's posture dwarfed in some way, so he straightened up on the chair and said in a constructive mood:

"We should post the information on the Internet. There are sites about missing people."

"I already did," jumped Adam. "Information and pictures have been shared on social networks all over the Internet."

"Nothing yet, I assume," said Mr. Nolan.

"No, nothing yet, but it's been just a few days and I'm watching it closely," replied Adam.

Silence filled the room again, but it wasn't as heavy as a few moments ago. Then Mrs. Nolan handed the ring back to Adam, saying, "As you said, this is for Gina. You'll give it to her."

"I will go now," said Adam taking the ring. He got up and said, "I will find her." And as he walked toward the door, he turned back saying, "I'm in contact with the embassy and Vatican police. As soon as I hear anything, I will let you know immediately."

When Adam left, Brian Nolan turned to his wife, "He is young, I am not, but I've never seen a man so broken up," he said.

IV

Months have passed.

At that time, Adam started work in the university's archives department. A job that he wanted, and which he got just before the Italy vacation. This was the first step to what he always wanted to get access to the sources, study original documents, and manuscripts, and view the historical events from the perspective of the people living in those times. Decrees of the rulers, declarations of religious leaders, their influence and the reaction of the society as a whole, or more or less organized groups of the people, and even records of seemingly insignificant events, less known facts, or facts not known at all, were all in his interests. And art was a big part of this historical puzzle for him, as he believed sculptures, frescos, paintings, music, lyrics, poems, stories, and pamphlets carried people's thoughts, and expressed their views and emotions. That could serve as a cause for some people's motivations, actions, and decisions, and at the same time, it could be very well the effect of those motivations, actions, and decisions for others. He knew this puzzle of connections, mutual influences, and dependencies could never be explained entirely, but this was his way to comprehend, understand,

and try to answer the question: Where do we come from? Or rather, how we became, who we are?

But now, all that excitement was gone. Adam participated in every aspect of the project as planned and expected and did all that was required to properly conduct the research, but he felt he was not involved as he thought he would be. His mind was occupied with Gina.

Sending emails and calling Vatican police or the embassy every few days produced nothing. All he got was the same answer, "Investigation is being conducted. You will be contacted if there is new development, or in the event we need additional information."

The web postings were equally fruitless. He scrolled through messages several times a day. Most of them were messages of compassion, support, and cheering up and helping by sharing and spreading it over the Internet.

One day a message caught his attention. Like many others it offered help, but not like the others declaring to spread the information, this one said, "I will help you find Gina. Contact me on the priv. Ariadne."

Adam ignored it at first, as it seemed as if someone was playing with him. So, he passed on the invitation. But more fruitless days passed, and he decided to give it a try. After all, it was standing out of the crowd, he thought, and not really believing it would lead to anything.

But Adam didn't want to feel like a complete sucker, so before he made contact, he asked Nick, if he could do some checking and find anything on Ariadne.

"She's a psycho, you should meet her," Adam read a message from Nick.

"Psycho?" Adam texted back and dialed Nick.

Nick answered the call, "What's up?"

"I've got your text. You said she's psycho," said Adam.

"Damn phones autocorrect," replied Nick and continued. "Psychic, not psycho. She's a psychic and from what I gathered she's really good. Sometimes she works with the police on cases of missing people. 'Sometimes' means she only gets involved in cases she feels for. She's weird. But if she contacted you directly, you should not waste it. She means hope. And she's here in Chicago."

"Thanks, Nick," said Adam and wanted to add, "you know, I'd do anything to find Gina," but the call was already disconnected.

Immediately, Adam contacted Ariadne and after they agreed on the price, they arranged the meeting. She insisted that Adam agree to the conditions put forth by her for the meeting to happen.

Rules were: First of all, she makes no guarantees or promises. He comes alone to her place. No cell phone or any other communication device, or any device able to take pictures or videos. He brings or forwards before the meeting, anything related to Gina. He brings an item belonging to Gina and also be prepared to answer any question, even intimate query about their relationship. Also, he brings the money in cash.

He agreed.

Adam knocked on the door of Ariadne's place at the set time. The door opened and as he walked into the hallway, he was encountered by a young woman with dark-framed glasses, and short, bleached, spiky hair. Fairly tall, she wore skinny jeans and a sleeveless shirt. Nipples of her breasts, breasts as he thought somewhat large for her figure, were sticking out through the fabric of the shirt. Her shoulders and arms were covered with tattoos.

"Ariadne cannot be her real name and she lets in a stranger just like that?" Adam thought suspiciously as he was walking in.

"Adam?" She asked.

"Yes," he answered.

"I'm Ariadne. That's my professional name," she said and added, "put your phone there and follow me," she pointed to the small table in the hallway, as she was certain he had the phone in his pocket.

"I also have Gina's phone. You asked to bring something that belongs to her," said Adam.

"Give that one to me," was the answer. "Do you have the money? You pay upfront," she added.

Adam was a bit reluctant, as he wasn't sure what he was paying for, but ready to do anything to find Gina, he pulled the cash from his pocket and handed it to Ariadne.

As they walked into the larger room, there were a number of computer and television screens hanging around, displaying videos, images, and different web streams with muted audio. Some of them Adam could recognize as news streams. Walking in, he was looking at that, somewhat surprised. "Now I'm sure she's got hidden cameras recording all this, or maybe even someone is watching us. That's why she's not afraid of letting strangers in," he thought.

"Is there something wrong?" Ariadne broke in, noticing his silent concern.

"No. I just…" mumbled Adam, still not quite sure why he was surprised and not knowing what to say.

But Ariadne continued, "You thought when meeting a psychic, you'll see a crystal ball and tarot cards? That's not how it works," and added, "we are safe, no one is watching us."

At this point, Adam let go of his reservations and calmly said, "I don't know how it works and I never thought about meeting a psychic and what to expect."

Ariadne seemed not to listen or pay attention to what he said; she set down comfortably on the couch in the corner of the room and kept talking, "Things come in from many different sources and different ways. Many ways are unknown, thus unaccepted. They crisscross, mingle, and rotate entwined, and twisted. Every turn creates an unlikely angle, a viewpoint showing something unseen before that perspective was created. Mostly it's invisible and untouchable. Every angle resonates different information."

In a way, Adam was moved by this, as he thought it was a performance, but kept serene and asked, "Can you help me?"

She got up and walked to the computer screen and pointing she said, "Come here. What do you see in this picture?"

Adam got closer and saw an image of a landscape.

"What do you see?" She asked again.

"Green hill," answered Adam.

"Anything else?" She kept asking.

"A sky with some clouds," Adam started to be annoyed.

"Do you see any people?" Ariadne kept going.

Adam at this point quite irritated, scanned the image up and down, side to side.

"I can't see any people in this picture," he answered with a tone of voice suggesting, he's finished with this game.

Ariadne touched the screen and slightly moved the picture changing the view angle on the screen. Then Adam noticed a shape surfacing in the picture, and as she kept turning the angle, a woman appeared in the landscape that was not visible at first.

"What you see now?" Ariadne asked rhetorically. "This is just a trick showing things really exist, but are invisible in two-dimensional space. When the third dimension is applied, multiplied view angles are available, and more can be seen. Believe me, there is a lot more crisscrossing dimension. Entwining and interactions of world and life dimensions create frictions affecting information warps. I only see viewpoints, others don't see. People call them visions."

"But can you tell me about Gina?" Adam asked, somewhat losing his cool.

At this moment, Ariadne 'woke up' from her altered state, as it seemed to Adam, and she stated, "Yes, I can tell you about Gina."

Then she turned around and got closer to Adam.

"Do you have anything belonging to her?" She asked.

"I gave you her phone and you have the pictures she took," answered Adam, somewhat confused.

Ariadne was looking at him in silence. Moments passed and he realized what she was asking for. It was not anything Gina owned or possessed, but what belonged to her. He understood… He reached into his pocket and pulled out the engagement ring. It set on his open palm and rested heavily.

Until this moment, he didn't think of it as being heavy. It seemed the presence of Ariadne made him think of it not as a joy, but as some kind of burden.

As they looked at it, deepening in their thoughts, Ariadne reacted first, "That's not hers. She never touched it."

Then Adam responded firmly, "But it belongs to Gina."

"Sure. You give it to her when you find her."

"I thought you going to help me with that," said Adam with a hint of frustration in his voice.

"I will try," answered Ariadne.

That intensified his feeling of disappointment, but he remembered—no promises. At the same time, he felt like opening up to Ariadne and voicing out something that he was afraid of even to let it surface in his mind. A thought that he was trying to push off all the time, but he said, "I even don't know if she's alive."

"She's alive," said Ariadne immediately.

At first, relief took him over for a second and then he jumped with excitement, "Where is she?"

"I don't know," was Ariadne's answer. And noticing how disappointment was taking over his excitement, she continued, "The pictures you sent me before, the pictures of the artifacts she took, I saw very similar images and they were touched by her very recently."

"Where is she?" Adam repeated himself getting more excited.

"I don't know. Come back another time. I'll let you know," said Ariadne.

"When?" He asked.

"Maybe tomorrow, I'll let you know," was the answer.

That night, when he returned home, Adam couldn't sleep. Feelings of anticipation and worry were fueling struggling thoughts in his mind. He was excited to learn Gina was alive, but on the other hand, was that information reliable? Maybe Ariadne played with him just to make her earnings valid? He recalled the situation when she showed him that the woman was invisible at first but revealed in a view from a different angle. She knew he was looking for someone that vanished, and I really wanted to see her. So, she showed him that trick. She played him well. But then again, she wouldn't tell him to come back. Yet, how many times has she said, "I don't know," "Maybe," or "I will try?" But then again, he remembered how surely, she stated that Gina was alive.

What will I do if she doesn't call tomorrow? It'd be easy. I just got scammed, he thought. "But what if she calls?" Still, he kept in mind that she said Gina was alive, and even though there was no proof, he hung on it and would not allow himself to think otherwise. He was determined to follow every lead, even if it would make him look foolish.

Ten days passed when he received a message from Ariadne urgently calling for a meeting at her place.

When Adam arrived, Ariadne seemed hyped up. She was dressed all in black. Black, long sleeve shirt buttoned up all the way to the neck and black tight leather pants. Dark make-up around her eyes and black lipstick. Only her hair was pure bleached, white. She seemed like a different person. Only the hair made her the same in his eyes.

As he walked in, she said, "I had a vision. It was on the news."

"Your vision was on the news?" Adam asked.

"Gina was…" Ariadne continued like she didn't notice Adam's question or his presence.

"Gina was on the news!" yelled Adam.

"Gina was in my vision and my vision was triggered by the news." Suddenly Ariadne calmed down. "Do you remember? The angles, interactions, levels, and visions? I cannot explain everything to you. You wouldn't get it anyway," and added, "have a seat."

"I don't need an explanation," said Adam sitting down on the chair, "just tell me about Gina."

"Gina is in Brazil," Ariadne said firmly.

"In Brazil? How? Why?" Adam asked.

"Yes, in Brazil. How and why, I don't know," answered Ariadne and added, "I knew you wouldn't get it."

"I'm sorry, I didn't mean… But I'm trying to make sense out of it," sheepishly said Adam.

"Making sense is not my business. I can tell you what I know," said Ariadne and continued, "that night, when you left, I was looking again at the pictures Gina took and kept looking at them, and kept looking at them… And I saw a message coming through. It was the message Gina was reading and I read it through her eyes. Rather it was some kind of prophecy. The images were distorted and intersected on many levels, making it difficult to see clearly. What I could see said: 'Church abandoned Europe. Then the church is saved and surrounded by speakers of similar, but different language, where Peter and Paul will be together in open arms of Jesus'."

Adam was stunned at the revelation, which really didn't make sense, so he only asked, "How does it make it to be Brazil?"

"There is only one country, outside of Europe, that is surrounded by countries speaking different languages, its Brazil. You see, Peter is the Vatican, Paul is Sao Paolo and there is the statue of Jesus with open arms in Rio de Janeiro. Gina vanished in the Vatican and as far as I can see, she appeared in Brazil."

But still not quite convinced, Adam asked, "You said it was on the news."

"Oh yes, it was on the news. They showed Muslim fighters destroying ancient temples and artifacts in the Middle East, smashing them into pieces. But looking at Gina's images, I saw her putting them back together."

"This is all confusing and I'm sorry, doesn't make much sense to me," replied Adam.

"Oh, really? It doesn't make sense? The world as it is doesn't make sense to me," answered quickly Ariadne. "I told you; I'll tell you what I know. Making sense out of it is not my problem."

The tone of her voice indicated it was time for him to leave. So, he got up and not really sure how to react to all of this, he said, "Thank you for your efforts. I will try to make sense out of it."

As he was walking toward the door, Ariadne stood behind him at the end of the hallway and said, "She's writing a diary; she wants you to find her."

He stopped, didn't turn, didn't say anything, and then walked out of the door.

V

Sunset, dark clouds seemed to be hanging oblivious against the gray sky, as the plane approached the landing path at the Sao Paolo International Airport.

Adam was looking through the window as the grid of lights and dark patches below were growing and forming into the shape of streets and buildings.

It was a month ago when Ariadne told him about Gina. He took that information to the police, even though he felt he would be ridiculed. But he figured—any lead was a good one. Police treated his information somewhat credibly, as they knew Ariadne from the past. However, she was involved in local cases. Reaching out to the authorities in another country was an entirely different ball game. Taking the report, they promised to contact the police in Brazil through Interpol. In the way, they were not discouraging, but gave him no hope, saying, "Brazil is a big country, you know."

So, yet again Adam took matters into his own hands. Not waiting for the answer from the Brazilian police, which as he had foreseen, never came, he reached out to his friend, Father Michael, remembering that he was on a mission in Amazonia.

The night they connected over the phone, at first conversation was usual and predictable. Adam mentioned Gina's disappearance and told the whole story of the fruitless pursuit through the proper, legal authorities' channels. Michael was truly sorry and offered his prayer. Then all changed— "I'm going to Brazil," said Adam. "Gina is somewhere in Brazil. Can you help me?"

"She's in Brazil? How do you know?" Michael asked.

"Psychic told me and I believe her. I'm going to Brazil and I'm asking you, can I count on you? And I don't mean the prayer."

"Now, hold on. You know, you're talking to the priest?" Michael said sounding somewhat upset. "You believe some psychic and you're asking a Catholic priest for help?"

"I'm sorry. No offense. But I thought I was talking to a friend. I'm sorry, I don't know what else I can do," replied Adam.

"No worries, I understand," answered Michael and continued, "I will be in Sao Paolo in two weeks, where missionaries of my congregation meet from time to time to discuss plans and progress. Please tell me more and how I can help?"

"If you could just meet me when I get there, it would be a big help."

"Yes, but why Brazil? Gina vanished in Rome?" Michael asked.

"The last message I received from Gina; she was in Vatican Museums. She was taking pictures of some statues being worked on. The psychic told me that her vision was triggered by the news of artifacts being destroyed and she saw a prophecy through Gina's eyes, and said Gina is where Jesus has open arms."

"What?" Michael interrupted.

Right then the connection was abruptly lost. After several failed tries, Adam gave up reconnecting. This in the slightest way didn't tick him to change his mind about going to Brazil.

In the next few days, he arranged a flight, booked a hotel in Sao Paolo, and dealt with other formalities. Then he had a conversation with his professor at the university and announced he was resigning from the job, as he could not predict when he'd be back.

To his surprise, his professor was very understanding and even supportive. He said he would do the same. And he would keep his position open for him as long as he can.

"Find your girl," Nick's words flashed through Adam's mind.

A day before his departure, Adam met with Gina's parents. He explained, without getting into the details, that he had dependable information that Gina was in Brazil, and as authorities didn't seem to be doing anything about her disappearance, he was going there to find her on his own.

They offered to help in any way they could, and they meant financially, but he refused and said if he needed any help, he'd contact them.

***

Now the plane was taxing, and Adam was thinking if he'd be able to connect with Michael. Not having a real plan beyond the next few days, getting in touch with him was Adam's only hope.

Going through customs and emigration turned out to be an experience. Adam was ordered to deposit digital fingerprints and his face and eyes were scanned. Seeing his puzzled face, an emigration officer with a barely noticeable smile asked in English, "What is the purpose of your visit and how long will you stay?"

Adam couldn't answer truly to either of the questions, so he lied, "I'm here for a month. I'm visiting a college friend and plan to see some parts of Amazonia."

"Your friend is Brazilian?" The officer asked.

"No. He's the Jesuit priest on a mission from the Vatican."

"Oh, I see. A priest."

Then he stamped the passport and handing it to Adam said, "Welcome to Brazil."

In the hotel room, the first thing he did after taking off his shoes and unpacking some of the necessary items, was to send a text to Michael, saying he was in Sao Paolo and wanted to meet. Adam simultaneously hoped for an answer and did not expect any. After a while, he went downstairs to a bar next to the lobby. He ordered a beer and still was hoping to get a message back, and at the same time convincing himself it would not arrive. Then, it did arrive. Father Michael asked him to meet the next evening and sent the address. Not knowing anything about the city, Adam showed the location to the bartender, asking for directions. The bartender looked at Adam's phone, then at Adam with a surprised look.

"You want to go there?" He asked with an accent.

"Yes. What's wrong?" Adam said noticing the bartender's doubt and added, "I'm meeting my friend there."

"That's not the area for tourists. But if you have a friend there… It's far, you take a taxi."

"I'm not a tourist," Adam cut the conversation.

The next evening. It was dark already. The cab driver stopped at the intersection and pointed to the right, to the uphill street lit by scarce neon signs. Adam started to walk the steep street almost in the dark toward the only light somewhere above. The narrow street soon turned into stairs with a visible yellowish light at the top. Coming up to the end of the stairs, he stopped. On the far side of a small square lit by the yellow bright light, he noticed four or five dogs chewing on something. Alerted by his presence, they stopped chewing and all of them gaped at him. Their stare frightened him, so he turned around and slowly started to walk down, thinking he might have to start running.

Still occupied with that thought, he got to the bottom of the stairs, when suddenly from nowhere or rather from the dark, four guys appeared and crossed his path. Adam stopped. Now he was really frightened. Then suddenly another figure appeared as if from nowhere. He walked closer and Adam noticed he was wearing a priest's collar and immediately recognized Michael. Michael turned to the other guys, and they also noticed his collar. He said something in Portuguese. One of them answered, and then Michael replied. After a moment of silence, as they were looking at Adam, they stepped away.

"Good to see you and thanks for saving me," said Adam still a bit trembling when they turned, and Michael led him into an even smaller street.

"Good to see you too," said Michael.

"In the hotel, they were surprised I wanted to go here. It's a bad neighborhood."

"It's not a bad neighborhood. It is a poor neighborhood," replied Michael.

"What was that about? What did you tell them?" Adam asked.

"I told them, you don't have what they want. One of them asked how did I know what they wanted? And I said it didn't matter what they wanted because you are like them—you have nothing." And then added, "Also, after all, there is still some respect for the man of the cloth here."

Michael led into a small pub, which seemed to Adam quite empty. He thought, *At this hour no people here?* There were a few people at the bar counter watching a soccer game on monitors hung above, but otherwise, the place was empty. Michael ordered two beers at the bar, and they sat at the table in the corner.

"I hung up on you when you called," said Michael. "I couldn't talk then… I couldn't talk about those things on the phone."

"I understand," replied Adam.

"Oh, you do? We can talk now. Nobody is here. They're not following anyone here, in those areas. That's why I chose this place."

"Okay, level with me," entered Adam. "I'm here to find Gina. She's got into some trouble, she disappeared, but I believe she's alive somewhere here. I'm here to find her."

"So, you believe Gina is here in Brazil? Based on some psychic prophecy?" Michael asked after a second of silence.

"Yes. I have nothing else to hang on to," answered Adam, right away. "Everybody I turned to since Gina's disappearance, only said they will try to help me, at best. This psychic was the only one that actually did something about it. I have no reason to doubt her."

After another short while of silence, Michael took a deeper breath and said, "Okay, tell me again what the prophecy said?"

"I don't know exactly. As I told you, the psychic conveyed only part of it. And she said she was looking through Gina's eyes at what Gina was reading. She said something like that: 'The church is saved in another country where Peter and Paul will be together in open arms of Jesus'. Then she said something about Muslim fighters destroying artifacts. And then, she said Gina is in Brazil, alive."

"The prophecy says," started Michael, "great evil from the east will come after the war. The church will abandon half of Europe. Church is saved, surrounded by speakers of similar but different languages, where Peter and Paul are together in the open arms of Jesus." And he continued, "This prophecy is so old, that the original version was lost and for centuries we only had a translation, a bad translation. Nobody really understood its meaning until after the First and Second World Wars. Then it made sense. Communism took over half of Europe and the church was saved in the western part of Europe. So, we thought. But we were wrong. Actually, the church grew very strong in Eastern Europe, even stronger than in the West. And very recently, the original manuscript of the prophecy was found in catacombs under St. Peter Basilica. Then correctly translated and we realized that it's not about communism. The prophecy said, 'after the war', but it didn't say when, or after which war. So now we understand the church abandoned Western Europe. You see, Peter is Vatican, Paul is Sao Paolo and Jesus with open arms is Rio de Janeiro," paused Michael.

"You know it? So, it's true. The psychic said that," interrupted Adam and added, "and the great evil?"

"What do you think? Just take a look at what's happening in Europe."

"Islam?" Adam asked.

"Their ultimate goal is to put the Flag of the Prophet over the St. Peter Basilica," said Michael.

At that moment, something clicked in Adam's mind and well-known facts and events began to take different shapes and looks. New meanings started to make more sense from this new perspective. For a second, Ariadne flickered through his mind, but then he knew he was not at that level, and he stuck to his own level of perspective. That meant recalling events in Europe's very recent history that involved church and Islam and seeing that in a different light…and shadows.

After a moment of silence when Adam somewhat digested that revelation, he said, "So, really they never gave up," recalling events of the siege of Vienna in 1683.

"Church is evacuating from Europe to South America," said Michael.

"But what it's got to do with Gina's disappearance?" Adam reacted.

"Church is evacuating from Europe, literally. My mission here is to establish new places of cult," continued Michael, like he hadn't noticed Adam's question. "You see, for the last few decades, Popes made concessions to Islam, especially on the theological level. At the Second Vatican Council, and after that, the church became open, but rather I should say, infiltrated with many ideas. One of which was ecumenism… You know, basically, that means, we are all children of the same God, but we express our faith in different ways, so all religions are equal, and we all just need to embrace our differences. Even atheists are considered to be lost children of God in this dogma. That made the church vulnerable. As it turned out, what was viewed as an opening and seemed a small and almost insignificant thing, was the basis for the downfall. Because only the church viewed it as reconciliation and embracing differences, but others like neo-Marxists, post-modernists, or whatever you want to call them, and especially Islam, saw it as a weakness and wasted no time to exploit it."

"So, the church is leaving Europe for grabs?" Adam broke in.

"No, actually the opposite, Europe abandoned the church. Or perhaps the church was taken from Europe. Europe is the root and was the center of Christianity since the beginning…" He paused for a second and then continued, "You know there is a passage in the New Testament: You are the salt of the earth. But if the salt loses its saltiness, how can it be made salty again? It is no longer good for anything, except to be thrown out and trampled underfoot."

"The church is moving its center to South America forsaking everything in Europe… And how is this being kept in secret?" Adam asked.

"It's not really a secret. Not being announced by the Pope or other Vatican officials doesn't make it a secret. People just don't care or rather don't pay attention to what's going on around them. And are being manipulated and occupied with things that are just diversions." Michael paused for a second. "You are aware of pedophilia in church? Everyone is…"

"Yeah?" Adam asked somewhat quietly.

"You see, the problem exists in the church, no one denies that, but… It's been blown out of proportion by the media. But the church with all its powers could at least limit this outrage. It didn't and there is a reason for it. People are occupied with those scandals; they talk, gossip, write about them, and even make movies. Some of that happened decades ago and nobody was raising a voice, but suddenly they're coming out. Tell me, were any of the perpetrators punished for what they did? Yes, some were convicted, but they're just the scapegoats to fuel public and media interest. Important, higher-up church figures— never. They're on it from the beginning. So, you see, people pay attention to things that really are not that important from the church's point of view in the whole scheme of things, and they don't notice things that are more important for the church as a whole."

"Like moving Catholic center to South America," added Adam, grasping the idea.

"Exactly, but not just that… It plays well with the new ideas and concepts, and planned changes in the church, like different views on celibacy and the role of women in the church. It's all planned and has been laid out during several synods, but not in the exact terms and details. But no one pays attention or cares anyway."

"Oh, my God. Is this for real?" Adam sighed as all he just heard seemed to come together and started to make sense to him.

"I'm telling you this only because I understand that your fiancé learned something and somehow got involved, and both of you could be in trouble."

"Yeah, I knew we were both in trouble since the day she disappeared. But how did she get involved?" Adam replied, and sort of changing the subject, asked, "But tell me, if it's all true, how do you deal with it, handle it? I mean, I always regarded you and still do as an honest, decent man. How do you deal with all that?"

"You mean the church business?" Michael asked rhetorically and continued, "Becoming a priest and joining the church as a priest is like marriage. You're falling in love; you are in love; it's great, exciting, and hopeful. There may be some kind of worry somewhere in the back of your mind, but not enough to stop you. And once you committed, there is no way back."

"All for the good of the church," said Adam with a notion of understanding.

"Do you want to marry Gina?" Michael asked, which seemed like changing the subject.

"Yes, I was going to propose to her in Italy," answered Adam.

"So, what if she changed after the wedding?"

"Change? In what way? We all change," said puzzled Adam.

"Sure, but I mean, in a way would that change your feelings about her?"

"You mean she'd go with another man?"

"No. That would be somewhat easy for you, am I right? What if she left you after the wedding, but not with another man? What if you were confused about her?" Michael kept asking.

"What?" Adam said and thought, *I'm lost, and I was looking for his help, but it looks like he might be lost too.*

"I mean, would it change your mind about her?" Michael continued asking.

"No, I don't think so. I'd tried to talk to her, understand," answered Adam without hesitation.

"But what if she left?"

"I see what you mean, but Gina didn't leave me. She disappeared."

"She disappeared from your world, your life. She's left you. But you're not giving up. You're looking for her," Michael continued.

"She wants me to find her," replied Adam without hesitation. "Gina wants me to find her. That's what Ariadne said."

"What? Who?" Michael asked, pulled from his state of thought.

"Ariadne, the psychic."

"Oh, that… Yeah…" said Michael, still emerging from his previous thoughts.

"Look, I'm a historian," started Adam. "What you're saying is totally interesting and I can understand to some degree the world of the church dogmas, philosophy, and politics, but for me, it goes far beyond scientific interests. I'm sure you understand that… That world directly affected me and my life, in a very strange way. I'm here to find Gina and that's all I care about. I know she got involved in it somehow and finding out how she is involved will help me find her. I must find her."

"I understand," said Michael. "But I don't know how to help you. I told you what is happening, but I don't know where Gina is. I'm sorry."

But Adam kind of ignored it like he almost didn't hear it, as his mind now was wondering about that odd way Gina's departure altered his life. That made him think that maybe this was a reason—to change him. But right then he tossed that thought. He needed to know how Gina could get involved. *If only I knew what happened,* he thought. And then he grasped what Michael was saying about church 'moving' to America and he recalled images sent from Gina's phone. Now he thought he understood.

But Michael broke Adams's thoughts of revelation asking, "What about that psychic of yours?"

"I'm not sure. She said Gina is writing a diary and she can read or view some of it. I don't know how and even if it's real at all, but she's said she'll be sending me whatever messages or fragments of the messages from Gina's diary she gets. She already sent me some." Then after the second of a pause, Adam continued, "Now, when you mentioned that prophecy, they could be real. I don't know what to think anymore."

Adam returned to the hotel room late at night. Now his belief that Gina was alive seemed obvious, but then again, that was just his assumption and his mind making a belief. He couldn't fall asleep. Thoughts of Gina were circulating in his mind, mostly questions filled with sorrow and remorse.

What's happening with you? How can I reach you? I want to hold you. Why did you leave me alone in this world? I miss you and whatever I do, I cannot get close to you.

Then, words from an old song they both liked came to him: *I want to take you in my arms forgetting all I couldn't do today.*

Adam decided to return to the States.

Gina

I

Gina was sitting in the quite large armchair encrusted with beautiful ornaments in front of an equally large and equally beautiful desk. She was trying to avoid eye contact with the man behind the desk but inevitably felt his stare. She tried to create an impression that she was debating on the answer to the question he posed to her a second ago, but she knew the answer right then and she knew that he did too.

Earlier that afternoon.

The door seemed to be locked, as Gina was pushing on it. After another push, it opened and she walked in, and immediately was met by the guard. "The museum is closed," he said.

Gina nodded, glanced around, and noticed the security camera above looking at the entrance. Then she turned around and walked back outside.

Standing in front of the entrance, she noticed a tour bus pulled up and people started walking out, forming a loose lane by the entrance. Group of fifteen or twenty people, all of them as she could tell were Asian, Japanese, or Korean, but some spoke English. It looked like they were getting ready to enter the museum. Seemed like some kind of special group tour.

She hesitated for a second and then mingled with the people in the group. She also noticed someone in front, a lady who must have been the guide. When the door opened and about a dozen people entered, Gina pushed through the lane and stood in front of another guard:

"I'm the guide," she said, "I'm late, I just can't find my badge, sorry." She smiled.

"The guide just entered," said the guard, looking somewhere behind him.

"Yes, she's the group guide, but more like a translator. I am the actual art guide," said Gina.

The guard looked confused, and rightly so. But in the late afternoon and at the end of his shift, tired, he just let it go and let Gina pass.

The group moved through the rooms of the museum led by the guide and Gina tagged along, without understanding anything the guide was saying. It didn't matter, she didn't care. At some point, the guide's voice just became like a subtle background, somehow kind of musical noise, and actually worked to Gina's advantage—she could sort of phase out and just enjoy the art she knew. The paintings, the sculptures, the reliefs, and the ornaments.

The art, the noise, the feeling, it was all beautiful. Seemed like heaven. And then it all suddenly stopped. They entered the Sistine Chapel.

There was no crowd, and the silence took over. Just silence, the art all around and above, and Gina in the middle of it. If all of what was happening before seemed like heaven, now, this was really heaven with the Garden of Eden just floating above her.

The silence wasn't really there, but it didn't matter. The outer world was muted by the mind. Standing there and enjoying every aspect of this space for the second time in one day seemed unreal.

But the reality was there all the time. Pushed out and swirled around on the fringes, but still, it was there. And then it suddenly entered and shuttered this perfect tranquility of the space and time…

It happened quite simply; the group guide just loudly ordered everyone to move out of the Chapel onto the next part of the museum tour.

As they entered, the guide announced and then repeated in broken English, "We are entering part of the museum, where pieces of the exhibition are under renovation process, and some may not be on display. Also, because we are on the specially scheduled tour late in the day, be aware that we may encounter museum workers moving some artifacts around, as part of this process."

Indeed, as they entered another exhibition hall, Gina noticed in the far-right corner a couple of men positioning a tall sculpture in a place using some kind of mechanical lift equipment. She moved closer to see what they were doing. Approaching them, Gina looked to the right, and through the open door, she thought she saw a very similar sculpture. Immediately, without any thought, she walked up to that door. She hesitated for a second and then entered the room, which turned out to be a quite large hall, warehouse-like type filled with crates, large boxes, and smaller boxes on the shelves. She noticed in a small distance the sculpture she saw through the opened door. A man using some kind of spraying equipment was covering it all around with something turning into a foamy and spongy-like substance. An uneasy feeling of suspiciousness got into her and trying not to announce her presence, she pulled out her phone and kept it at the waist level, and with shaking hands started to take pictures. While taking pictures, Gina noticed in the distance to the right some strange machine that looked like it was painting something on the canvas. She realized what it was, as she wrote about it in one of her college papers and in an article for an art magazine. Then suddenly, someone behind her yelled something in Italian.

Gina put her phone down and right into her pocket, turned around. She was looking at the man approaching her quickly.

"I'm looking for the restroom, ladies' room," she said nervously.

The man stopped, looked at her, and after a short pause asked with an accent in a loud voice, "Who are you? What are you doing here?"

"I'm with the tour. I was looking for the restroom," and immediately corrected herself to be understood, "I'm looking for toilets."

"No toilet here. You must go," said the man and added, "no one is allowed here," almost taking her by the arm walking with her outside the room, repeated, "You have to go."

"Where are the toilets?" Gina asked to keep up her story of being lost.

"You go there," the man pointed ahead. "Then to the right. Go to the end. There is a sign."

Still suspicious, the man called his superiors.

Gina went and walked fast, following the man's instructions, turning corridors and passing hallways. She knew he was not following her, but it felt like he was right behind her. At one point, she was passing the sculpture she saw that had just been replaced. She stopped for a second and got really close; she could almost touch it. It seemed to her that it was delicate like new and never seen before. But the feeling of being followed and watched took over and she made head quickly for the restroom.

The restroom was empty. Gina stood in front of the mirror but did not look at it. She was looking down at the sink. She turned the water on and immediately shot it off. She looked up facing the mirror... "I stumbled on something, and I think I know what it is," she said to the face in the mirror. "Do I?" She added.

She took a deeper breath, pulled up her phone, and sent the pictures she had just taken in that room to her cloud account. Walking out of the restroom she thought, *When I get home, I'm going to take a closer look.* Then Gina started to look around for the possible way her group might have gone. She noticed a couple of people disappear around the corner in the long hallway. She went in that direction, but she only made a few yards, when two men appeared as if from nowhere in front of her.

"Where are you going, miss?" One of them asked.

"I was in the restroom, and I thought I was lost, but my group is over there," said Gina, pointing at the end of the hallway.

"We are museum security and I'm afraid you need to come with us."

"But where and why?" Gina protested.

"We will explain. Can I have your phone?"

"Why? What's the problem?" Gina kept asking but she already knew what the problem was. She saw something she shouldn't have and took pictures of it.

"We will explain," said the man and demanded, "give me your phone now," and added, "please don't make us use any force."

Gina pulled out the phone and handed it to the man.

"Now come with us."

One of the guards was leading the way and the other was right behind her. After several turns and not too long a stroll, it seemed to Gina they left the museum, and she'd be released, but when they walked through the tall and large door which the first guard just opened for them, she walked into the room and that feeling disappeared. Gina entered a space without windows surrounded by tall shelves holding hundreds of books, old volumes with decorative letters picking through the glass doors. Shelves and doors themselves were encrusted with decorations embedded into the wood. This room looked like one of the rooms in the museum, but with one small difference, it's being used.

"Please sit down," said the first guard, pointing at the comfortably looking large armchair in front of the large desk with some papers and documents spread around a big monitor and the computer keyboard.

"Someone will be here shortly," said the guard, and then they left closing the door behind them.

II

Gina was alone in the room, sitting in the large chair, more like a sofa, that indeed turned out to be comfortable, but she understood, her situation was not. Time was passing and nothing was happening. No one was coming. At least, half an hour passed. Sitting and waiting, Gina was looking around the room surrounded from three sides by books. Only the wall behind her had two tall shelves in the corners filled with books. The rest of the wall was occupied by the three sixteen or seventeen-century paintings, from the first look, framed in ostentatiously decorative, gold-plated frames. She got up to look at them closer. Looking at the paintings from some distance and then from close, they were in the 'El Greco' style, however, they were not his, she decided. After a while, Gina moved on to walk around the room looking at the books and other artifacts on the shelves.

As she went around the desk, looking at the idle, blank computer screen, she thought she needed to return to the pictures on the wall. Something made her think about the middle painting. And as she was looking at it, she realized that it was a painting she saw in the catalog of paintings lost during the Second World War. As much as she tried, Gina could not recall the painter or the title and thought, *How did it end up here?* And for some reason, she answered herself, "Some Nazi thug paid with it to escape justice."

At that moment suddenly the door opened, and a man dressed in a black suit entered the room. He noticed Gina standing and looking at the paintings and he said, "If you think it is El Greco, it is not."

Surprised Gina turned around to face the man and pulled herself together rather quickly, and said, "I know. But I'm thinking about the painting in the middle."

"Oh, I see," answered the man after the short pause, like he knew what Gina was thinking. "You could be right, but it was here before my time." And added walking to the desk, "Let's talk about our time. Please sit down."

Now Gina noticed his somewhat German accent. She moved closer to the chair but did not sit.

"On what grounds am I being detained? I am a U.S. citizen. Give me back my phone and release me immediately," she demanded.

"I'm afraid I cannot do it," answered the man sitting down.

"I will be missed by my group," said Gina still standing, like she was going to leave any second.

"You and I know that you will not be missed by that group, as you were never part of that group," said the man and repeated, "please take a seat."

As she was sitting down, she asked, "Where is my phone? I need to call my boyfriend and let him know where I am."

"I'm afraid that's not possible either. And I don't have your phone."

"What?" Gina almost shouted. "My phone was taken by the security and you, the chief of security, don't have my phone?"

"The chief of security has your phone. I am not chief of security. However, we work closely together," said the man.

"Then who are you? Whom am I talking to?" Gina asked surprised.

"My name is Karl Langen. I oversee a very special project here at the Vatican." He paused for a second and added, "But as I think about it, for me it's more like a mission."

"I'm detained because of your project. What do I have to do with it?" Gina inquired.

"Please allow me to explain," Karl paused for a moment and continued in a somewhat relaxed tone. "We watched you from the moment you tried to enter the museum this afternoon. While you were waiting here, we checked who you were. We have the means. We know everything about you, and I realized we share a common passion for preserving art. You saw something that you shouldn't have, and you know what I'm talking about. And that's why you are here."

Hearing that, Gina felt somehow comfortable, but still some nagging, worrying feeling was lurking around her mind.

"And my boyfriend? He will be looking for me, he'll go to the police, authorities…" she said.

"I'm sure he will, but he'll never find you," answered Karl.

Now that worrying feeling hit her with full power and that bit of comfort, she felt was gone in a second. She was terrified.

"What are you going to do?" She jumped.

"Look, Miss Nolan," said Karl with a significantly serious tone of voice. "You don't understand the seriousness of your situation, because you don't know what is at stake here. So let me put it plainly," and he continued with the previous lighter tone of voice, "you have to disappear, and you will disappear, but whether you survive your disappearance or not, it's up to you. Did I mention we have the means? I'm giving you a choice and proposition to work on my project. I am giving you the opportunity of your life."

Gina was scared and confused. Questions were running through her mind. What would they do if she refused? Would they harm her and in what way? What exactly does he mean by 'disappearance'? How would she disappear? Obviously, death came through her mind too. And what about Adam? Would they harm him too?

And at the same time, she was drawn into the thought of this 'lifetime opportunity'. She knew it had something to do with preserving the art, but she was confused, how was the project of preserving the artifacts tied to her life or possible death?

"What is the project you'd like me to be involved in? What will I have to do?" Gina asked.

Karl all the time with the stone face, seemed to smile a little. But his smile was almost invisible, so Gina could not be sure.

"Saving the greatest art collection in the world."

"But why do I have to disappear?" Gina asked still confused and scared.

"You'll know everything if you agree to get fully involved and I'm sure you are more than capable. Otherwise, there is no point in telling you any details," he said and added, "so, what is your decision?"

Trying to avoid eye contact, she was feeling his stare. And as she tried to create the impression that she was debating on the answer, she knew the answer and she knew that Karl did too.

Gina looked at him and said, "So, it's like in the 'Godfather' movie, you gave me an offer that I can't refuse."

Then Karl added, "I'm glad we understand each other."

"Yes, I want to survive. I want to take this life opportunity," said Gina.

Karl was definitely released, it showed on his face and Gina noticed that.

"I believe you are serious about your commitment and that gives me peace," said Karl.

"Gives you peace? But I'm not in peace. What about my boyfriend?"

"You have two loves in your life. You just answered yourself, which is most important for you."

"But he won't give up on me," replied Gina.

"Yes, I know that."

"He'll go to the police. He'll tell them I went to the museum," Gina continued.

"I know he will," said Karl. "But we have a surveillance video showing you entering the museum and being turned down by the guard and exiting the building. And we'll inform them that you left the premises, and since then, your whereabouts are unknown to us." And added, "Believe me no one will question Vatican's security and investigate us further."

"Promise me, you're not going to hurt my boyfriend," said Gina.

"I promise we'll be watching his movement and actions, but we have no quarrel with him and have no intentions of hurting anyone."

Then he got up and said, "Please follow me and I'll show you your temporary living quarters."

"Temporary?" Gina inquired.

"Yes, temporary. Please be patient, I will explain everything. We can start discussing it later at the dinner, or late supper, rather." And added, "Do you have any special requests for your meal? I know you are a vegetarian. I'm sure we can arrange it."

"Looks like you know everything about me," replied Gina, trying to hide to be surprised.

"No, I don't know everything, but I knew enough to make you the offer I did," said Karl, showing the way out.

Walking along with Karl down the hallway with walls decorated with ancient frescos and old furniture along the corridor, her thoughts, mostly questions, were rushing through her mind, *They know a lot about me, but not everything. How much do they know? I am to work on a project that I know nothing about, but he says, I am a good fit for it. Why am I good for it? Why me?*

"Here is your room," said Karl, suddenly stopping and pointing to the door on the right.

As Karl pushed the door open, Gina entered quite a small room. Noticing her hesitation, he said, "Please, it's not a prison cell; it's just a quick and temporary solution."

"Not a prison cell, ah?" Gina replied boldly.

"Please understand we did not expect you. Behind that door in the corner is a bathroom," said Karl and continued, "unfortunately, we cannot provide any change clothes for you at the moment; we'll try to arrange it as soon as possible. Please, make yourself comfortable here; someone will let you know when the supper is ready."

The manners and kindness of Karl got Gina a little more comfortable, but then again, she still was being held captive against her will. But now she just wanted to settle and recoup her situation, and this room seemed well suited for that, so she said, "I'll be fine here."

"And for your meal?" Karl asked.

"Nothing special, some greens and bread will do. Thank you," answered Gina.

"Not a problem. Now please relax, if you can," added Karl, then turned around and left the room closing the door behind him.

Gina stood in the middle of the room, nicely decorated with old paintings on the walls, the desk and the chairs, and the sofa.

Try to relax, she thought sitting down on the sofa.

III

Gina got up off the sofa, walked up to the door, and opened it. Somewhat surprisingly, it wasn't locked. She peeked through and as far as she could tell, there was no one in the hallway. The hallway was kind of dark, but to the right, it seemed to be a little brighter. She ran down toward the lighter side but realized that running might seem suspicious if there was anyone watching her. So, she halted and walked slowly toward the light. *But then again, who would be watching over me?* She thought. As she turned right again toward the light, she entered a gallery-like room and became surrounded by ancient sculptures floating around and hanging like in-the-air paintings. They were crossing each other's paths in three dimensions, showing up from nowhere and disappearing into the unknown. It was beautiful beyond words. And at the same time, it was an unreal experience.

Until now she was always looking at art, but now all the art was looking at her. Wherever she went in that realm, whatever angle she tried to look at those art pieces, it was as if they were looking at her, as if she was the center of the exhibition. Some sadness seemed to be creeping into that space, but not quite realized and defined. And still, it felt like a pleasant and comfortable position to be in.

It was not real.

She was pulled out of this unreal world by a knock on the door…

"Miss Nolan…" She heard a voice from behind the door. "Miss Nolan, dinner is ready."

Gina awoke.

Just a dream, a beautiful dream, and a weird one too, she thought sitting up on the sofa. She felt the sadness of the awakening, but somehow delight of the dream was still streaming into reality.

"Miss Nolan!" said the voice behind the door again.

"Yes. Give me a minute," answered Gina.

"Yes, Miss Nolan. When you are ready, please take it to the right when you walk out of your room. The hallway is lit and will lead you to the dining room."

"Thank you. Will do," answered Gina.

The splash of cold water on her face was refreshing and as she walked out of the bathroom, she walked out of that dream entirely.

Opening the door and walking out of the room felt like in that dream, but she knew now it was for real. She turned right as she was told, but really there was no other way. Then she followed the walkway lit by the light, and then again turning right. And it might feel like in the dream, but in the dream walking down the corridor seemed kind of like striding down. Now this one was evenly leveled. It was real. The door at the end was opened, so she walked into the dining room. Solid, heavy, large wooden table in the middle of the room lit by the huge crystal chandelier above it and by the light coming from the candelabrums hanging on the surrounding walls.

At one end of the long table, Karl was sitting, and he got up as he noticed Gina walking in.

"Hello, Miss Nolan. Please take your place at the table," he said, showing the other side of the table, where another table setting was prepared.

"Just the two of us for this dinner tonight," he continued, "as I said, we did not expect you," and added, "but rather, I should say, you surprised us. But please, let's eat, and let's talk."

Gina walked to the table sat down and said, "Yes, let's talk."

Someone showed behind her and placed a plate with green salad in front of her, as well as a basket of fresh, warm bread.

"As you requested, green salad and freshly baked bread," said Karl. "Anything to drink? Wine? White? Red?" He asked.

"Thank you. Just the sparkling water," answered Gina and added, "tell me about the project."

"Oh, yes the project," said Karl and asked: "Don't you want to eat first?"

"I eat and you talk," said Gina decisively.

"As you wish. So… The project is a very special project of art preservation and restoration," started Karl as Gina was reaching for the glass of water.

"And you kidnap people for that?" Gina boldly interrupted him before taking a sip of water.

"I said it's a very special project. Please be patient and you will understand," answered Karl in a way that made

Gina kind of sorry for interrupting. And Karl continued, but somewhat offbeat, "I know what you're thinking. There are dozens of art restoration people working in Vatican Museums and you're right, but they don't work on this project. They even don't know it exists. This special project involves restoration and preservation techniques, and processes, but the art objects are not returned to their original places. They are being relocated and preserved. The originals are being replaced, and this requires secrecy. I'm sure you understand the originals are replaced with almost indistinguishable replicas. The public cannot be alerted in order to keep the preservation process flowing. The preservation has a different meaning here."

Gina as surprised as she ever was, just asked, "But why?"

"Hordes of barbarians have been entering Europe for quite some time now. Some are even invited by Europeans. Things like that of course happened before in history, but never on that scale. A couple of decades ago, the church decided to leave Europe, I mean physically leave."

"Abandon churches and people? The church is the people too?" Gina asked.

"Europeans abandoned the church and Christian ways of life a long time ago," continued Karl. "And don't be mistaken, when I said 'barbarians', I didn't mean just the Muslims who entered Europe, and not even those that were here for decades. I meant all those forsaking, opposing, and even fighting Christian values and our way of life. Those are new barbarians."

Gina was listening in silence, as she was grasping the idea and reasons, not just for the situation she was in, but overall, the state of the civilization she grew up in and was part of.

Karl broke the moment of silence, "Are you interested?" and continued, "You see, if it wasn't you, we'd dismissed the whole case as an unfortunate accident of someone entering restricted areas and no one would notice. But you… You have a talent, skills, and passion for preserving art. I cannot dismiss you."

Gina was interested and now kind of flattered by Karl's view of her. As she was absorbing all that Karl was saying and remembered what he said before, it seemed a bit annoying at first, as she already agreed to be a part of the project and was willing to follow through. And then she understood, her agreement was somewhat imposed on her. Now, he wanted the agreement of her own will, even though that was the only choice she had. He wanted her to believe it.

"I already agreed to be part of this project and I have not changed my mind," Gina broke the silence. "But I see you don't believe me."

"Not true. If I didn't believe you, we would not be speaking tonight. We can get back to our beliefs at some other time. But now, please allow me to continue on the project," replied Karl. "As I said, we, the church are evacuating from Europe. As opposed to what happened before, you know, like leaving Constantinople centuries ago, this time we are not going to leave our most sacred and valuable artifacts behind. We are committed to preserving our heritage. Those barbarians would destroy it. The way we're doing it is to recreate artifacts and replace them with identical pieces for the display, then transport the originals into the new environment, and reassemble them in settings identical to the original environment. Basically, we are moving the Vatican physically to another place on Earth. Everything under cover of restoration."

"Where?" Gina asked.

"South America, the remote interior of Brazil," said quickly Karl.

"Brazil?" Gina replied with surprise. "You are going to move the Vatican to Brazil?"

"We are already doing it. You'll see. You will participate in that process," said Karl with contentment in his voice.

"I see," said Gina and yet again sounded like she knew, she really had no choice and Karl seemed to notice that and said:

"I see you are committed, but not quite convinced," and continued, "did Michelangelo have a choice? He was more of a sculptor than a painter. How was he convinced by the Pope to paint the Sistine Chapel? We'll never know. We know he was not enthusiastic about this job at first, but we see what he has left us with when he committed to it."

"Excuse me," entered Gina abruptly and somewhat firmly, "you are not trying to compare me to Michelangelo?"

"Absolutely not, I'm only presenting similar situations."

"Similar situations? You are taking the original art pieces, moving them to an undisclosed location, and replacing them with the fakes. You are asking me or rather making me to participate in the forgery?"

"Technically, it is a forgery, but in reality, it's preserving the real art from destruction for future generations," answered Karl expecting another uphill battle.

But to his pleasant surprise, Gina said, "I'm convinced and committed. Let's discuss work details and environment."

"Yes, let's do that," said Karl, trying somehow to disguise his relief.

"Yes. I understand we're not going to be able to discuss all the details now, but can I tell you my immediate needs, so I can do the work? Starting tomorrow?" Gina said and added, "It ties to the work environment."

"Yes, of course," said Karl and was quickly cut off by Gina.

"I need new clothes and other personal use items, like toiletries and such."

"Sure, we know that. As I mentioned many times before, this situation is a surprise for us. But I was assured by our IT department that by tomorrow you'll have our Internet access and you'll be able to purchase anything you need, and it will be delivered the same day or the next day," explained Karl.

"Thank you," said Gina.

"But as far as the work environment, you have seen it, but not quite, if I may say so," said Karl and added, "but as you wish, we can wait till tomorrow."

Gina noticed a little smile and the hint of teasing secrecy in what Karl just said, and asked, "What do you mean? What work environment?"

"Would you like to see where you're going to work?"

"Where?" Gina asked.

"The Sistine Chapel. Would you like to see it now?"

"Now?" Gina jumped. "Any time," she added right after.

Karl got out his phone, pressed a button, and after a second said, "This is Karl, can we come in now? Yes, thank you." Then he got up and turned to Gina with a smile, "Shell we?"

The door was slowly opening. They walked into the well-lit Sistine Chapel. There was no one there, just Gina and Karl. The silence was overwhelming. Gina felt like ascending to heaven. She looked up and stared at the ceiling, and the feeling of immersion into the creation had returned, but this time it surged much stronger. Gina knew she was in heaven.

Karl noticed that in her eyes. He wanted to say something but didn't want to ruin what seemed to be perfect music.

Gina glowing from that apparent state of silence turned her eyes down to him and said, "There is a haven."

"Do you believe in saving heaven for future generations?" Karl asked and after a moment he added, "You can spend as much time as you wish here. Outside of tourist visiting hours, of course."

Karl started to go back to the door. When he got there, he turned around and said to Gina, "About Michelangelo, you know the first sculpture he did and sold was a forgery." Then he walked out, leaving Gina alone in the middle of the chapel.

Standing there and looking up again she was truly convinced and committed, and one thought gripped her mind—*I am being held hostage, but now it's not against my will. On the contrary, I am the captive of my own will. Is*

*that a faith? Am I becoming a believer? In any case, I will
do everything I can to save it and protect it.*

IV

Knocking on the door awoke Gina. At first, she thought it was part of the dream she had; dreaming of being captured and locked somewhere in the Vatican. In the dream, she was wandering, how come she never thought and tried to escape? And now she's waking up from the dream, waking up to her true reality. When the knocking repeated, she was awakened and certain it wasn't a dream, and the situation she was in, was real.

"Who is it?" She asked.

And the woman's voice answered, "Breakfast will be served in a half hour if you'd like to join us. The same room you had dinner last night."

"Thank you, I'll be there," said Gina, and immediately thought about what she would be wearing, the same clothes she'd been wearing for the last two days.

Gina walked into the room lit by the morning bright penetrating the stained-glass windows. There were people sitting at the long table. They surely noticed her, but there was no movement. They were still and silent. Then, Karl sitting at the end of the table lifted his head a bit and said, "Dear Lord, thank you for bringing us together this morning and blessing us with this meal. Blessed be those who prepared it and all who will share it." Then he turned his eyes to Gina. "Gina, welcome," he said. "We're all glad you're here. Please sit down with us."

Besides Karl, there were five people at the table, three men and two women. As she could tell by their appearance, they were of different ethnicities. They turned toward Gina as she was approaching the table, and Karl continued, "This is Gina, a new member of our team."

They all turned friendly smiles toward her and a few said, "Welcome."

Gina smiled back and picked a place almost at the end of the table and somewhat separated from the rest of the group, as she did not feel quite part of the team yet. She felt more comfortable being a bit distanced, for now. But as she was sitting down, she felt everyone gaping at her.

"We all read the article in the *Art Science* magazine on your idea of fresco preserving method. We think it's brilliant," said someone.

"What was brilliant, the article or the idea?" Gina asked.

And as she was sitting down, Karl got up and pointed to Gina's chair, he said, "The idea, of course," and then, he continued, "and we are grateful the idea is represented in the flesh." He smiled and added, "Let's eat."

As everyone was reaching for the food on the table, talking, smiling, and gesturing to each other, Gina felt content and watched as the coffee was poured into her cup, even though she didn't ask for it, she thought, *They like my idea. These people, strangers like the idea of preserving art.*

"We'll need to take it a step further," said Karl, directly to Gina, pulling her out of her thoughts.

"A step further?" Gina asked.

"Yes. We will put it into practice and implement it in the real world. We are all here to help and you tell us how. We'll discuss details at the meeting before lunch."

***

Gina went back to her quarters tired, just thinking of lying down and resting. All-day meetings, discussions, explaining the process and details of something that was just an idea. A well-thought-out idea, but still an idea. All of that drained her down. But at the same time, she was excited to be able to put that idea into practice and use it in real art. And what art it is.

Walking into her room, she noticed right away a man by the desk leaning down above the laptop on the desk. He noticed her too as she walked in and stood up and appeared not even a bit surprised.

"Who are you? What are you doing?" Gina asked.

"Hi. I'm Sebastian," the guy replied quickly and continued, "I've brought your laptop and set you up on the network."

Sebastian was a tall guy with long thick black hair, neatly combed back. Just a good-looking guy in his early thirties and well-dressed. His eyes seemed to stare at Gina through and out of the dark-framed glasses he wore. He did not look like a computer geek to Gina.

And as she was getting closer, approaching her desk, he said, "I was just setting it up. I was going to come back later to walk you through the process," said firmly Sebastian.

"No, we can do it now, if you have time," Gina replied quickly, as she felt revived, and her tiredness just went

119

away. "Show me," she commanded sitting down at her desk.

"It's very simple, nothing out of the ordinary," said Sebastian, leaning over. "Just log in with the password of your choosing. It can be anything and then you're on. You can search and browse anywhere and anything."

"Anything?" She asked.

"Anything," said Sebastian.

"I meant the password," replied Gina.

"Oh, yes, the password can be anything. Anything meaningful and memorable to you," said Sebastian and added, "I'll look away as you enter it."

"Why?" Gina asked. "I'm sure you can get it from the system at any time."

"You're right, we can," answered Sebastian without hesitation and added, "but I don't want to know. I do not care," and he continued, "once you log in, you can access any website, and interact just as normal."

"Just as normal? What do you mean?" Gina asked.

"Interact as normal, just as I said," Sebastian got somewhat upset and serious, as he saw this question was intruding on his work, which he considered his world.

Gina noticed that and tried to ease the situation and said, "I just want to order a few items online. Can I do that?"

"Oh yes, absolutely," said Sebastian calming down. "I see you might be tempted to communicate or use the system to broadcast to the outside. However, communication is controlled; you can see them, and they can see you, but it's only virtual versions of you and them. And that's easily controlled."

As he said that, Sebastian felt somewhat self-vindicated, and it showed. And he continued, "We call it 'Hall of Mirrors', it is a net of virtual instances of the sites, objects, images, communications, and messages that only exist virtually. Well, they only exist virtually any way."

"Double virtual?" Gina broke the silence and added: "Is this for real?"

"Yes," answered Sebastian with some sadness in his voice.

Noticing that Gina asked, "You call it the Hall of Mirrors? That's the title of the song by the German band Kraftwerk."

"That's right. That's how I came up with the name for our network. I like Kraftwerk. You know them?" Sebastian got excited.

"Yes, I know Kraftwerk. I like German electronic rock of the seventies," answered Gina.

"So do I. But those times are gone now," said Sebastian and saying as he sinks back to low-key mood from his temporary enthusiasm.

In his mind, he recalled his younger days when he was part of a group working on the different concepts of the Internet and alternative approaches to interactions and communications. That thought got him into a nostalgic and somewhat sad mood, as he knew; some of his colleagues were more prosperous working and implementing those ideas for corporations and in some cases for the governments. But then again, otherwise he would not be, he could not be part of this particular project. One of the biggest projects in the history of our civilization. And that feeling of being part of something bigger than life was his compensation for anything else.

They didn't know each other, but in a sense, they were similar—they found themselves in very much the same situation. Both were working on the same very interesting project, coming to it somewhat reluctantly, but convinced of its importance and truly committed to it.

So, Gina realized that she didn't want to exploit it further. Although some part of her was different and that part took over and made her pursue another path—the path of questioning the system setup and maybe, getting somehow outside of it. She thought she could in some way play Sebastian and his knowledge of the system to get him to connect with the outside of the network and reach Adam. So, she started camouflaged as innocent and asked, "Who is 'we'?"

"What?" Sebastian replied.

"You said, 'We call it Hall of Mirrors' Who is 'we'?"

"'We' I meant our IT, network team," said Sebastian, regaining his reality.

"Oh, the team?" She said, realizing her futile position as there were more people involved. "I'm going to rest now. I'm exhausted," she added.

"Oh, yes. I'm sorry, I'm leaving now," said Sebastian and quickly walked out of the room.

And as he was walking out, Gina asked, "Sebastian…"

"Yes?" He turned around.

"Do you have cameras installed and connected to your systems?" She asked.

"Of course, we do, but not in this room. No one is watching you," said Sebastian and added, "you're safe here."

***

Gina entered the room where the team usually had a dinner celebrating milestone achievements in the project. But this time there was only Karl sitting as usual at the head of the table.

"Gina, please have a seat and join me," said Karl getting up off his chair and pointing to a chair on the corner next to his.

"Is anyone else coming?" Gina asked, noticing only two dinner placements on the table.

"No, just you and I," answered Karl quickly and added, "please sit."

As the dinner was being served, Gina asked, "Are we celebrating something? Usually, we all get together here for some celebration."

"Yes, we are. We'll get to it soon," answered Karl. "But now, please tell me what you think about the project. I mean its progress. It's been months you spent on extracting and preserving the art in its original form."

"Well…" Gina gathered her thoughts, "As unexpected as it happened, I believe it turned out to be a good thing and it's going quite well."

"Yes, it is going quite well," confirmed Karl, "and I believe it's time for you to leave."

"Leave?" Gina jumped. "What do you mean? Leave now, in the middle of the project?" and at that moment, she realized what that would mean for her, and just thought to herself, *He's going to let me go free? No way.*

And right then, she got the answer.

"Your work seems to me completed here," started Karl. "I know there is still a lot to be done, but it can be continued by someone else on your team. You implemented your idea, and you trained them well," he paused for a second, "I'd like you to work on re-assembling the real art in its new home."

"In Brazil?" Gina interrupted.

"Yes," said Karl without a second of hesitation.

"For a moment, I thought…" whispered Gina to herself.

But Karl picked that up, "You thought I'd release you, let you go?" and he continued, "With all you know and your commitment? Yes, knowledge and commitment. I know you are committed to this project and the knowledge serves you well."

At that moment, the conversation kind of stopped, as dinner was being served. The staff knew both guests' tastes; there was plenty to choose from. But Gina's mind was not quite on the food at this moment, so trying to continue the conversation, she asked, "You said my knowledge and my commitment. What about you? Is it the same?"

There was a little pause, as Karl was taking food from the serving plates to his plate and was making sure that the serving staff left the room, and then he said, "For me, commitment came before knowledge." He cut a piece of meat and put it in his mouth, chewed on it, and then he took a sip of wine.

Gina was looking at him without saying anything. She didn't want to break the moment, as it looked like Karl was about to tell the story, his story.

"I'm from a small village in Bavaria. I was a little boy." Karl set the stage for his story. "Every week I was going to the Sunday mass at the church, Catholic church. At a very young age, I became interested in the art, paintings, mainly paintings displayed all around the church walls, and then the mass itself. Later when I grew a little, but still a child, I'd go to the church more often, but still more to admire the art than to attend to the creed."

Gina stopped eating and turned her attention to Karl's story, as she thought it was just a prelude, and rightly so. Karl continued, "Church was not the only place that I was surrounded by art. I was born and grew up in a home where old paintings of some of the best artists of the past were hanging on the walls. They were just like those in the church. That was my grandparents' house, which they share with us."

Karl paused for a second.

"My grandfather was an alcoholic; most of the days as I remember, he was drunk, but that day, that particular day was different. There was no one around, just him and me. Drunk as usual, he started to take the paintings off the wall, bringing them outside, putting them on a pile, and lighting them up on fire. I didn't know what was going on, but as the first paintings started to burn, he'd go back to the house to bring more of them. I could not stand watching the paintings go up in flames. I ran into the house, I took down all that was left and I ran with them to the church to save them. I was then maybe eleven, maybe twelve years old, still a young boy…"

Karl paused again, looked down, and said, "That day I saved the art from destruction. That day changed my life. I put myself on a course to preserve art."

Then he looked up at Gina, and again took a sip of wine.

"No one knows or doesn't want to admit they know, where and how my grandfather acquired all those paintings. Later, growing up, I learned that my grandfather was studying art and wanted to be an art history teacher. When Germany started the war, he had to join the army. He was sent somewhere in Eastern Europe. After the war, when he returned home, those paintings appeared in his house. Now I know where they came from."

Silence took over the room.

"I know, Nazis looted and destroyed art all over Europe," Gina broke the silence.

"Nazis?" Karl jumped. "Nazis?" He repeated and went on, "Please spare me. Look what it says on the gate to the Auschwitz death camp. It's in German. It's a German concentration camp. In occupied territories, there were signs on the buses, restaurants, and theaters saying, 'Nur fur Deutches—Germans only'. Hitler in his speeches always talked about Germany, the German people, and the German Lebensraum, the living space for Germans. Nazism is the murderous ideology created and carried out by Germans. Please, don't be fooled."

Now the silence really fell and expanded slowly settling across the room. Gina wanted to break that silence and wanted to say that she understood and that she was sorry, but she couldn't find the words, and in the end, it turned out she didn't have to. Karl had it first:

"Don't feel sorry," said Karl like he was reading her mind. "I know my grandfather was not a Nazi; he was German like I am. I don't know much about my grandfather's life. We never talked about our family's past. Maybe what he did during the war led him to drink and that after the years led him to the rage and burning of the paintings. Maybe it was the way he tried to deal with his past. Was he burning his memories? I don't know." Karl ended.

Gina felt like there was nothing more to say when Karl said, "But don't be sorry for me. What happened cannot be erased and I'm not here to deny it or even justify it, as some other Germans try to do. On the contrary, I'm here to testify against evil and do what I can to stop the spread of destruction," and after a second, as he paused for a breath, he added, "you can put that into your diary."

"My diary?" Gina's first thought was to question and protest of intrusion of her privacy, but then she accepted the fact that Karl knew about her diary and concluded that there was no point in making a big deal about it, as she figured he didn't care what was in it, and she didn't care he knew.

After the moment of silence and changing the subject entirely, she said, "When am I to move?"

"As soon as possible," answered Karl quickly, never cut off guard from the main topic. "But you tell me when you are ready, and I'll make sure everything is set and arranged for your travel and arrival," and then he added, "do not delay."

V

Gina walked into the meeting room; no one was there yet. She was alone. She took her usual place at the table. After a moment, the other team members started to enter the room and take their seats. And as they did, they were looking at Gina, feeling as if she was in charge of that meeting. Then, Karl walked in, took his usual seat at the head of the table, and said, "How is everyone?"

At that, everyone relaxed, but Karl continued, "According to our plans, we reached the point, where we are ready to move our operations to another location," and after a second of pause he added, "to our destination."

Then he turned his look at Gina, obviously passing a baton to her.

"As we all know, our destination is to preserve art," started Gina. "Our goal and our destination is to preserve art from destruction. As you know the destruction of art has many faces—natural elements in the air, and so-called natural elements, but really the pollution is created artificially, and then there is deliberate destruction enforced by people who have quarrels with other people. We are involved in all of those but with emphasis on the last one."

What Gina said was not exactly what Karl was thinking and referring to, but he was silent and tried not to show his slight surprise and concern. She noticed that and moved on with the explanation, "Our project is to preserve art and if preserving means moving that art to another location, this is what we oath to do. As you all know, the new destination for this art is very far from here and now came the time to embark on that phase of the project. Some of us will stay here and some of us will travel to that destination."

Gina paused and turned back to Karl, "Now, we shall discuss the details of our plan."

Unexpectedly as it might seem, Karl easily took over the meeting and explained without hesitation to each team member their role in the next phase of the project.

And as he was going on, Gina was noticing people's reactions and how without the words, however noticeably, they expressed their feelings.

Some felt discontented, some disappointed, as they may have hoped for something else on that journey, but they all accepted their tasks and the place. They all knew what they had signed up for.

But while Gina was observing the room and looking at her colleagues confirming acceptance of their roles in the next phase, she was thinking, who volunteered for this project and who was persuaded to volunteer, like she was? Nevertheless, she concluded that all, including her, were certain that what they were doing was the right thing to do and even more, it was necessary to do.

***

Faint lights were shimmering over people sleeping or just napping in their comfortable seats on this charter plane flying over the Atlantic. It seemed like Gina was the only one quite awake. She was reading her latest entries in the diary.

"I'm scrolling through the list of artifacts, numbering and identification of fresco pieces, proper labels and proper packaging of art that was sent on the freight ships to Brazil. I hope all will arrive safely soon after our team gets settled at our destination."

Gina recalled one of the last meetings with Karl before the departure. He mentioned art pieces collected from other significant places of Catholic cults, churches, and museums throughout Europe that were also packaged and shipped with Vatican art.

She remembered him telling how they were acquiring important paintings, sculptures, and devotional articles under the cover of restoration, and replacing them with fakes. At one point he smiled and said, "In some cases, we arranged to be asked to restore the artifacts."

When Gina showed surprise, Karl quietly added, "Do you really think the fire at Notre Dame Cathedral in Paris was an accident?"

Yes, he was right, as only the roof suffered significant damage, and they were able to secure and lay their hands on the most important pieces when they were asked for restoration expertise.

"Now, the Shroud of Turin," continued Karl. "It's such a controversy. Some say that it's real, and some that it is fake. It was under the scrutiny of various scientists who tested it using different methods, and the results were inconclusive. I think I know why. As it was moved from its original place and from one lab to another lab several times, no one really knows what they're examining. But in any case, we have the original."

Karl seemed to be carried away by stories of his accomplishments. But for Gina, just for a moment, a thought zipped through her mind, connecting Karl and his grandfather, robbing the owners of their possessions, which meant more to them than the market value of the art. And that prompted her to ask, "So, what about places of pilgrimage where miracles are believed to occur and they hold vital relics, which in many cases are exquisite pieces of art?"

"Those, we'll have to abandon," said Karl as his smile disappeared. "But just the artifacts, those places, and relics will need to serve faithful believers as they did for centuries," said Karl with full seriousness and added with some sadness in his voice, "these are the true beacons of our religion, and we cannot take them away from the faithful. That is something we cannot forge or replace."

He paused for a second and then continued, "Now, came to my mind the Santiago de Compostela, a true, real-life symbol of stronghold against the enemy. Yes, fallen, but not conquered, then rebuilt and a place of pilgrimage for centuries. People walked on foot hundreds and thousands of kilometers to reach this place."

And Gina imagined people walking on hot and dusty roads, taking refuge in the shades of the trees and resting in the dark thickness of the night. They didn't have many possessions with them, but the load they were carrying was quite heavy. Blessings, remorse, thanksgiving, prayers for health and well-being for themselves and those close and dearest ones, and anything they thought was so important and, in their minds, worth undertaking this journey, this sacrifice. They carried the load of their lives.

Am I lifting the load of my life, taking this as my journey? Is my sacrifice worth it? What if I fail? Is failure even an option? Enduring is the key here, she thought.

Then Gina's thinking was cut off, as Karl continued his talk, "That place and places like that is a promise. Before the journey, people promise to get there and the place promises that when they reach it, the purpose of the journey will be fulfilled."

And he added something irrational, but logical by his standards, "That cannot be forged. It's not even imaginable to replicate billions of footsteps along hundreds of kilometers of the roads."

Gina understood Karl's logic, but she knew his character by now. He'd do anything if he could to reproduce those footsteps. Perhaps even make people walk those roads again to achieve this goal. If only he was provided with the means, he would not hesitate.

But as she recalled that conversation, some thought occupied her mind now.

"The promise," Gina thought. "So, the place we are going to is like the promise. It is the promise to us. And once we get there, then what?" And after a moment, she answered herself in a content mood, "What we are doing is not just a promise to us; we are building a promise for others."

As she was thinking about the well-being of the artifacts, she felt everything was in order and in place. Then suddenly for no apparent reason, her mind switched its attention to Adam, or maybe Karl's words about carrying the heavy load and things not replaceable led her mind to it.

Was really everything in place and in order? She thought. *Adam's worry and fear that he certainly must have gone through, and the burden that my vanishing put on him. That was not in order,* she thought.

Gina wrote in her diary. "Adam, there are only two loves in my life. One is you and the other is art. I can only be fully faithful to one, the other will be betrayed. I thought, I made the right choice before, but now, it looks like life on its own made another choice for me."

For one shortest moment lasting less than a second, like a vein of electrical current, almost unnoticeable, but firm, a thought ran through her, *If I choose Adam, I wouldn't be able to fully spread my wings. That would be a waste of my potential. Would that be a waste of my life?*

Then she put another note in the diary. "I cannot even imagine what I have put you through. If that means something to you now, I am sorry. And I mean that."

And as she recalled the conversation with Karl, she wrote, "There are things that cannot be replaced. One of those is love. True love cannot be replaced. I made a choice, and I am guilty of betrayal. I chose to spread my wings. Adam, please understand me. You know how torturous this is for me. I don't know what else I could say… Please, understand me."

VI

It was morning and the sun was shining over the tarmac as the plane was taxing to the isolated hangar at Sao Paulo airport. Gina opened her eyes just a minute earlier.

So, this is it. I'm here, she thought. *But I was thinking about another world, the world I left. Was I dreaming?*

Gina wasn't dreaming and even if she thought she was, it was time to wake up. So, she did wake up to her new life, forgetting old dreams and with positive encouragement, that the world she left would be seen again and that she would make that vision and that world would come true. At that moment, the optimistic feeling was so strong that even the smallest, single thought of that vision being of a distant landscape, could not blur a bit.

In an upbeat mood, Gina got off the plane, got on the charter bus taking her and the rest of the team to the site, and she knew that this was just the beginning of the realization of the plan to restore for the future the world she left.

After a few hours of traveling through the countryside roads, they arrived at the site. The view was impressive. For a second, it seemed to her like she was back at the Vatican. But when they walked in, it was dull and empty.

"It's empty," Karl stood by her. "That's where you come in," he added.

"I will put the life here," said Gina still having in mind the vision and her feelings about it.

"I was hoping you'd say that, and I know you can do it," smiled Karl.

Walking with Karl through the huge, empty, but promising space, her vision was sinking more and more, and she realized that accomplishing that goal required more than her enthusiasm. What was needed to make it real was the experience of previous generations. Generations that created and built the original.

"We need more. Hundreds of years more," said Gina to Karl.

"Yes?" Karl answered a bit puzzled.

"We need more than we have," continued Gina. "If we are going to make this the real place, we need to know the reality of the life of the times when it was originally created. The frescos, paintings, and sculptures are expressions and representations of life, people's beliefs, aspirations, achievements, longings, dreams, fears, demons, and downfalls… Something that describes the reality, space, and atmosphere of those times. Art is just a channel that provides that insight."

Karl looked at her and some kind of understanding transcended from him when he said, "That's your fiancé's forte, am I right?"

Funny, he thinks of Adam as my fiancé, but Adam never proposed to me, thought Gina.

And she was ready to ask to bring Adam on the project, but she knew it was not possible and Karl confirmed that right then when he said with a real sense of seriousness in his voice, "That's outside of the scope of this project. You know it and you already made your choice." Trying to soften the situation, he added, "I know it's not easy for you. I understand how difficult might be to forget, but we've made a promise and that made us committed." And then he added, "You already spread your wings."

That was another reference to her diary, and it wasn't surprising.

As Gina thought that ended her slight chances, the task ahead of her grew to the size of mountains and the end of them was disappearing beyond the horizon, then Karl broke the silence and her thoughts.

"I think we might have something that may be useful to you. Let's settle down here and we'll talk after."

That triggered Gina's curiosity, but Karl stepped out and said, "We brought some books, manuscripts, and papers. We are transferring the Vatican secret library here and most of that collection is already here. That's part of another project that we're not involved in, but it's part of the whole. The 'secret' is an exaggeration; most scholars have access to all published documents in that library. However, only very few can read those unpublished materials. If you need to use those in our project, I have secured full access for our team," and he continued, "the guide will take you to your quarters and I'll get you there. Let's say in a couple of hours. Is that enough time for you? But we can postpone it till tomorrow if you wish. Most of your work is not scheduled to start for another few days."

"Yes, I know," said Gina. "But I should be ready in a couple of hours."

"Excellent," replied Karl. "I'll see you then."

At that moment, some young girl plainly dressed appeared out of nowhere and politely pointed for Gina as if asking to follow her.

***

The travel and the excitement were bearing on Gina in a strange way. She felt tired and sleepy. As she made herself comfortable in her new room, she lay on the sofa, but at the same time anticipation of something big was preventing sleep from really taking over her, so she was just resting there with her closed eyes.

A sudden knock on the door woke her up from the half-sleep state.

"It's me, Karl. Are you ready?"

Gina waking up recalled they were going to see other areas of this enterprise that could help in her project.

"Yes, sure," she yelled out. "Give me a couple of minutes to refresh. I'll be ready shortly."

"No problem, no rush," said Karl.

Stepping up the stairs, they walked out into the enormous space that Gina almost immediately recognized as a St. Peters Cathedral. It was huge and empty. Enormous and empty space, but filled with noises generated by construction machinery, equipment, and workers. Though that seemed tiny in this huge space, the noise they generated seemed to fill the space.

"You didn't think we were the only team building this place?" Karl said walking in front. "We are just a small group of many working on this endeavor. There are architects, engineers, builders, and construction workers. Most of them don't know what we're building and to be honest they don't care. Only some of the top people have knowledge of what is being created here. They are committed as we are."

"That is sad," thought Gina. "Most of those workers don't know what they're working on, but what's really sad is that they don't even care."

Gina and Karl were walking across the floor to the other side; she could see that people were doing what they were told to do, what they were supposed to do without any reflection or consciousness.

Passing by the moving trucks and construction vehicles, Gina noticed a huge crane, but it was not even reaching halfway to the ceiling.

Karl saw as she was looking up in awe and amazed, he said, "It's scaled one to one. Yes, it's huge, it's so huge, and you could fly a helicopter here." He smiled and continued, "I was here only once before, it's quite a progress they made here since then."

"They don't know; thus, they don't care," said Gina.

"What?" Karl asked, as the noise of the machines interfered with his conversation.

"Nothing, it doesn't matter," replied Gina.

They reached the other side and walked into the narrow hallway, Karl turned to the closed door on the side, and opening it he entered a dim corridor. Gina felt some discomfort going down the barely lit stairs, but she followed Karl. Soon they entered the large chamber.

"There should be a light switch here at the door," said Karl, and reaching out to the side he turned the lights on in the large room.

The lights went on and they found themselves somewhat dwarfed at the door of a huge warehouse-like space filled with boxes and items of different sizes stocked up on the shelves arranged in alley-like paths.

"So, this is Fabbrica di San Pietro, a Dream Archive," said Karl.

As they were walking along the shelves, looking and the endless volumes of manuscripts and books, Karl continued, "Not everything is here, but what's here has been cataloged in the searchable database and is available to us as scanned documents. Many documents and books are not scanned yet but are referenced in the catalog. Those you can retrieve and view here."

"Oh, yes. And I'm sure they all are in English," joked Gina.

Karl almost laughed. "No. But there is this robot-scanner-translator that you can use. I don't know how it works and how to use it, but I'm sure you can easily figure it out."

They entered a small office-like area with computers and monitors all around. It was a bit dimmed, but monitors produced enough light which created a fine, tranquil setting for reading and viewing old documents.

Then just behind them a woman showed up quietly and asked, "Can I help you?"

They turned around and Karl said:

"Hello. We are from the Sistine Chapel restoration team. I'm Karl and this is Gina."

"I'm Renée," said the woman.

She wasn't tall, but being filigree suited her well. She looked in her late twenties. Black, thick hair reaching the end of her neck. Dressed in a dark and not quite business-like suit, but still elegantly fashioned. Her pale face was quite a contrast with her dark hair and her suit.

"I'm managing this facility. Everything that comes in and out, and how it's handled," continued Renée.

"Nice to meet you," said Gina.

"They call me the robot lady because I set up the scanning robot and database system for the archive."

"Great," exclaimed Karl. "We may need your assistance then. Gina is leading the restoration project and she may need to look up some original documentation preserved in the archives."

"Sure, no problem," replied Renée. "What do you need?"

"Oh, nothing at the moment, I just arrived and I'm looking around what's available to help our team with the project."

"I see. I can show you how the robot works, and you can come here any time, and use it when you need it. It's quick and easy."

Renée stepped up to one of the monitors and started to explain the document retrieval process. "You can use any of these computers here. They are all tied to our searchable database."

Gina and Karl got closer, and Renée continued, "On this screen, you simply type in the search box or just say what you're looking for. It works somewhat like a search engine, but this one is powered by our own AI and only searches our catalog and includes so-called 'info-lineage', a display in a graphical way of the information requested, so you can tap into that information at any point in time and space of its existence."

"Everything in the archive is cataloged, however, not every document or book, or manuscript is yet scanned. The search engine searches every word of scanned documents. The result screen will show found documents and their physical location in the archive. You know, the location, the shelving number, etc. If the document is scanned, you can view actual scans, as well as translations. If there are no scans available, then the robot comes in. You click or say 'Retrieve'. The robot goes to the proper location, and pulls the requested document... It can handle every type of document—scrolls, single sheets of paper, and books; it can gently turn the pages in the books. It can even get stone tablets and papyrus. It scans them and translates them at the same time, and then sends them to this screen. And of course, all of it is registered and processed in and by our AI algorithms."

"That is just incredible. I'm sure it will be a big help in our project," exclaimed Gina.

Renée smiled. "As said, you don't need to use the keyboard, you just touch the screen, or say what you're looking for, it's all there," and Renée looked at Karl.

They all understood that the keyboard was for old-timers, like Karl. Karl agreed with a friendly smile and said, "I know what you're thinking. But what's next? A direct link to our thoughts?" He said philosophically, and he smiled again.

"If you need anything, I'm in the office next door. Now, I shall leave you," said Renée.

"I see you like it already," said Karl to Gina. "I have a few things to take care of now, but you can stay here if you wish and play with your new toy," he added with a smile.

"Yes, I'll stay here for a while," answered Gina.

"All right then. I'll see you later tonight at the dinner with the rest of our group. You can find your way back, right?"

"I think so."

Karl left and Gina stood there alone looking at the computer screens. But she was not alone. She stood there together with the machine. The machine that had access to history. The computer screens were not ordinary screens, now in her mind they were getaways to a different, new world. To Gina, it felt very symbolic and poetic—she herself was in the new world and standing in front of another world, but those were in the past. No, she was not alone. She was amazed and excited, but she was not quite prepared for what was ahead.

Images, texts, and images of the texts, books, and scrolls were just pouring into the screen, as Gina barely typed a few letters in the search box on the screen. A list of possible word strings as a new option showed as well, just asking to be clicked to display links to more options. Each window on the screen offered access to the original document, its location, images, translations, and more viewing and accessing options for the viewer.

It was like a dance or a ballet, as she imagined images and words dancing on the screen. Sometimes erratic, but mostly in sync with the music in her head.

"Amazing technology," she thought.

Then a more conscious side of her mind made her ask, "Sistine Chapel," and after that, she chose to see documents.

Looking for some kind of blueprints or some design documents resembling those, while scrolling through, she noticed in the list an option to view Pope Letters. Suddenly, she remembered Adam talking about the exchange of letters between the Pope and the Polish king during the siege of Vienna. So, she had forgone her own search and asked the machine to display library content about the siege of Vienna. The screen filled up with links and Gina was stunned. She wasn't sure if this was her mind influencing the computer or the other way around, the machine read her thoughts, and it seemed like the AI applied, but in any case, the first links on the list were to the Pope's correspondence with the Polish king.

Adam was right, she thought. *There was direct communication between the Pope and the king before the siege.* And as she was just glancing over the letters, it was obvious that the Pope was urging and at some point, even bagging the Polish king to come with aid to save Christendom and Europe from the Islamic invasion.

Then she went on reading other documents and for some reason asked to show the recorded prophecies.

Documents in the form of images display rotating on the screen in the fashion of a slowly turning carousel, with titles and keywords hanging above and ready to be selected.

First appeared prophecies of St. John's Book of Revelation. As Gina read some words and sentences, she imagined horrifying visions of the hail and fire mingled with blood, plagues devouring lands, cities, and the inhabitants, and eternal condemnation in the depths of hell.

With an aversion, Gina thought to herself, *Terrifying apocalypse. I should have known better, that's the most known prophecy.*

Then she stopped at the old black and white photographs of children standing in the field. The label above said: Fatima. And Gina said to herself with disappointment, "I know that one too." So, she flicked through some more items in the search results displayed showing letterers describing papacy deviations and thought with sadness, "Death, destruction, plagues, debauchery, and final condemnation. One word encompasses it all. One word: fear."

Then another thought came to her, *Escaping the fear, was the theme.*

And then, she realized that all those prophecies end with peace and tranquility in the Kingdom of Heaven. God is always triumphant. And she recalled a sentence, she read a few minutes ago from the letter sent by the Polish king to the Pope after the Battle of Vienna. It was a paraphrase of Julius Caesar and it said, "I came, I saw, God conquered." That made her think about Adam again. Uncomfortable for some reason with that thought, she pushed it away and looked at the computer screen. There was an image of some handwriting labeled 'Peter and Paul New Church in the Kingdom of Heaven'. The word 'New' triggered her curiosity. She selected it. The screen displayed side by side the original handwritten letter in Latin, and translation in English. It read, "Church abandoned Europe. Then the church is saved. The new church arises in a place where it is surrounded by speakers of similar, but different languages. There Peter and Paul will be together in open arms of Jesus in the Kingdom of Heaven."

The realization was obvious, and it came to Gina embodied in one line. "St. Peter, Sao Paulo and the statue of Jesus opened arms in Rio."

"So, that's why we're here in Brazil," Gina concluded.

This conclusion changed her mood to be a little calmer, as digesting previous texts and visions made her quite upset. Now she knew she could concentrate on the project with a better understanding and with a larger perspective.

***

At dinner, Gina took a seat at the table across from Karl. She calmly sat down. Looking at each other he knew that she knew the prophecy. Without a word and only with a hint of a smile that merely appeared, but more in their eyes than on their faces, the understanding was mutual. But she noticed some unease in Karl's face.

The long trip, time adjustment, and eventful day lay heavy on Gina, but what happened at the end of the day and the calmness at the dinner table, good food, and wine made her relaxed. It was a good feeling, and she was ready for a sleep. She said good night to everyone and left for her room.

In the middle of the night, Gina seemed to wake up to some noises behind the door of her room. She saw some kind of movement and some shadows in the light coming through the crack at the bottom of the door. She thought she heard some voice but could not make any words out of it. At first, she thought it could have been some cleaning service moving through the corridor. But at some point, she thought she heard Karl's voice. Then suddenly she heard a loud noise like a helicopter flying nearby. She immediately made a connection to what Karl said about the vastness of the basilica, imagining a helicopter flying inside that building.

She tried to get out of her bed to find out, but then someone behind the door, and Gina for some reason imagined it to be Karl, spoke in a loud and dark-sounding voice, "I possess you from the beginning. Incubating your true love. Oh yes, I use love, but not like He does just for himself. I use it to free people not to enslave them. I brought you to Rome to spoil the so-called manifestation of God's love, the great art. And you fell for it. I did it to save you. But He uses you and those like you. And at the end, He laughs at you, because he doesn't care for you."

After a moment, it continued, "You should know, all those artists struggled and suffered unbearable torments and misery. Rejected, cursed, and pushed beyond limits and they still gave everything they had and more. They were failures to the world, but in death, they were glorified and saved. Just like you. You gave up everything dear to you, but in return you got nothing. But I'm here and I will save you. So, in the end, you will preserve and prolong me. Take a closer look at what you are doing. What you are extending, and proliferating is me. Yes me. My name is Death and thanks to people like you, I am alive. I am appearing in thousands of pieces of art that you are preserving. Look closely, I don't play a supporting role. I'm a central figure. The good fights against evil, but ultimately death wins. Death conquers both. So, in the end, all portray me and thus propagate me, the Death. I am the shadow of every move you make. I am alive in you."

Then suddenly everything stopped and before Gina opened her eyes, she knew it was just a bad dream. The loud noise coming from the outside was the sound of tropical rain. Gina got out of her bed and stood by the window. The darkness outside was only broken in some spots by dimmed lights surrounding the area. The light was hardly coming through the water literally pouring from the sky even through the thickest canopy of the forest, soaking everything around. To Gina, water coming from the shower in comparison seemed to be just a little trickle washing off some sweat. What she was witnessing was a pure force of nature in the form of life-giving water. She'd never seen anything like it. She was dazzled by the sheer, naked power of life.

Felt safe inside her room, maybe just a bit frightened. She thought the scare may have come from the terrible nightmare she just woke up from, which now returned to her mind. As she recalled the dream, she thought, *What am I really doing here?*

Gina went to her desk and opened her diary. Remembering the dream, she started to write.

"Visit to the library, the Vatican secret library. I read an old prophecy that said, the new church will be established where Peter and Paul meet again. I'm here, where St. Peter meets St. Paul in the new world, trying to save the old world. I thought I knew why, but I'm not sure anymore that the old world needs to be saved or even wants to be saved. I had a dream that tore me apart. I feel like one of those people painted on the Sistine Chapel ceiling ripped between heaven and doom. Pulled down to the abyss by what seems to be a new and righteous thing to do, and holding on to what's above and old, but not quite clear. It all stopped making sense. I never thought it'd be that way. I don't know what to do anymore."

Gina recalled part of the dream about the artist tormented while alive and saved by death, sometimes suicide death and she thought about Adam's affection for Van Gough. She knew that for Adam it wasn't as much for the paintings, but rather how the misery of life was transformed through Van Gogh into the beauty of his art. And that is how he was saved forever. So, she added in the diary.

"Can I be saved? Is anyone ever going to read that? Adam, please find me."

The Beginning and the End

Adam cries out in his sleep.

"I read your diary!"

Then suddenly he wakes up.

It was a dream, he realized. *All of it was a dream, just a weird dream*, he thought.

It's before dawn; sitting on the bed, Adam looks over and Gina is sleeping aside. He relaxes completely.

As he calmed down from that terrible dream, he slowly realized that he recalled everything so vividly, not just the places, situations, but people, conversations, and dialogues that he was not even a part of. They were coming to him so clearly that for a moment he wasn't sure if he really woke up from that dream. But, looking over and seeing Gina sleeping in the bed next to him, he knew he wasn't dreaming.

Adam got up from the bed making sure he would not wake up Gina. He quietly closed the door to the bathroom, turned the light on, and stepped into the shower. Reaching out to turn the water on, he hoped the sound of the flowing water would not wake up Gina sleeping just behind the thin wall of their small apartment.

Standing in the shower he thought, *What a dream it was. It was like a dream from one dream to another dream and within yet another dream. I was dreaming Gina's dreams.*

Absorbing the water flow seemed like a way of cleaning off the night's state of existence, but he wasn't sure if he wanted to really be that washed off. Part of him wanted to revel in that unreal part of the dream.

When he was done with his shower and put the towel on, Gina walked to the bathroom.

"Did I wake you up?" He asked.

"Yes, but the time is up. We need to get ready, we are leaving soon," said Gina sitting on the toilet.

Adam left the bathroom saying, "I know. We don't want to be late for the airport. Italy is waiting."

Through the closed door, Adam said to Gina, "I had a really weird dream. You betrayed me."

"Oh, have I? What a dream?" Gina answered through the door and added, "With whom? Was he tall and handsome like you?"

"You betrayed me with your true love, the art. In that dream, I gave up everything for you, and you gave up me," said Adam.

"Wow, that must have been some dream," she said.

"Yeah, I know. We weren't married yet, but like today we were going to Rome. I was going to surprise you and propose to you there."

"Really? That would've been nice," replied Gina.

"But you disappeared in the Vatican Museum to save the art," continued Adam.

"I could definitely disappear in the Vatican Museum," joked Gina, but with some excitement in her voice and continued, "I could vanish there without a trace, but I would not be lost."

"You were writing a diary and I could read it as I was dreaming your dreams."

"That is really creepy," said Gina and added quite insensibly, "have you been drinking last night?"

"Not joking," replied Adam and added, "I'll tell you all about it on the plane. We're going to have a lot of time then."

Adam started to put his clothes on and said, "You went to bed early last night, but I finished reading your paper on using the newest technologies to preserve artifacts. I think you have really good ideas. Actually, quite revolutionary ideas."

"I know," yelled Gina through the door, completely unemotionally, which was typical of her.

As she was getting into the shower, Adam said, "Before I went to bed last night, I got a message from Father Michael. He says he will meet us briefly when we arrive, but he cannot be our guide and spend much time with us. He's going to South America, Brazil on some kind of a mission," and added quickly, "that was in my dream too."

"There goes our guide," said Gina as she turned the water on.

"I know. We'll have to find our way around," said Adam and continued, "in my dream, all of it was not real. Not dreamlike, unreal, all the art was not real, it was all fake. Do you think what we're going to see there is true and real?" He paused and after a second, he said, "I guess we'll have to find for ourselves what's true and real for us." And he didn't mean the art in the Vatican Museums, and he added, "There are no guides."

But Gina was already in the shower, water was flowing, and she couldn't hear him anymore.

The End

Poet, prose writer, screenwriter, and multimedia creator, born in 1965, in Poland. Jarek Tomszak lived there until the mid-1980s. Since then, he has lived in the United States. He has published three volumes of poetry in Polish: *Awakening, Decades*, and *Comet in Coma* and two collections of short stories: *The Official Version* and *The Last Horizon*, which was awarded the 'Golden Kościej Award' in 2019 in the category 'Short Story of the Year'. He also wrote short stories and screenplays in English. His film *Showroom Dummies* was awarded at the Slamdance, an online festival of experimental short films. *The Eden Evacuation* is his first novel written and completed in English.